BY BRET ANTHONY JOHNSTON

Encounters with Unexpected Animals

We Burn Daylight

Remember Me Like This

Corpus Christi

Naming the World

ENCOUNTERS WITH UNEXPECTED ANIMALS

ENCOUNTERS WITH UNEXPECTED ANIMALS

stories

BRET ANTHONY JOHNSTON

RANDOM HOUSE
NEW YORK

Random House
An imprint and division of Penguin Random House LLC
1745 Broadway, New York, NY 10019
randomhousebooks.com
penguinrandomhouse.com

Hardback ISBN 9780399590153
Ebook ISBN 9780399590160

The stories in this work were originally published as follows: "Paradeability" (*American Short Fiction*), "Soldier of Fortune" (*Glimmer Train Stories*), "Encounters with Unexpected Animals" (*Esquire*), "Caiman" (*AGNI*), "The Beginning of Wisdom" previously titled "Republican" (*Ploughshares*), Miss McElroy (*Ecotone*), "Young Life" (*The Southampton Review*), "Dixon" (*Virginia Quarterly Review*), "Playing the Ghost" (*Texas Monthly*), "Palomino" (*The Southern Review*), "Time of the Preacher" (*Virginia Quarterly Review*), "Half of What Atlee Rouse Knows About Horses" (*American Short Fiction*)

Printed in the United States of America on acid-free paper

1st Printing

FIRST EDITION

BOOK TEAM: Production editor: Ted Allen • Managing editor: Rebecca Berlant • Production manager: Richard Elman • Copy editor: Madeline Hopkins • Proofreaders: Claire Maby, Barb Stussy, Al Madocs

Book design by Ralph Fowler

The authorized representative in the EU for product safety and compliance is Penguin Random House Ireland, Morrison Chambers, 32 Nassau Street, Dublin D02 YH68, Ireland. https://eu-contact.penguin.ie

In memory of Mike Anzaldúa,

and for Joe Wilson, Cheryl Pfoff,
and Vanessa Furse Jackson,

and for Julie Barer

verifiable. Have I
included the memory
of the animals. The animals'
memories. Are they
still here. Are we

—Jorie Graham, "Are We"

CONTENTS

Paradeability 3

Encounters with Unexpected Animals 29

Soldier of Fortune 35

Palomino 58

Dixon 66

Young Life 93

Playing the Ghost 111

Miss McElroy 120

The Beginning of Wisdom 134

Time of the Preacher 161

Caiman 180

Half of What Atlee Rouse Knows About Horses 185

ENCOUNTERS WITH UNEXPECTED ANIMALS

PARADEABILITY

Serious clowns have their faces painted onto blown-out goose eggs. My son tells me this on the drive from Corpus Christi to Houston. The custom began in the sixteenth century, a method of remembering makeup patterns, but now it serves as copyright. The eggs are done up with acrylic paint and accented with felt and glitter, with tiny flowers and ribbon and clay, and the records are preserved in the Department of Clown Registry in Buchanan, Virginia. He says a clown's makeup is called his slap, and whiteface clowns rank highest in the hierarchy. Then the augustes, with their red cheeks and ivory mouths. Then character clowns, then hobos. The first known clown appeared in a pharaoh's court during Egypt's Fifth Dynasty—he was a pygmy. Clowns in Russia carry the same clout as pianists, as ballerinas.

It's a tepid Friday in March, and we're going to a clown convention at a Marriott by Hobby Airport. On Sunday he'll compete in a contest hosted by Clowns of America International. Asher is thirteen. He's a hobo.

"Fear of clowns is called coulrophobia," he says. He's paging through one of his clown books in the glow of my truck's interior light. Outside, the dusk is particulate. We cross the Brazos

River, rust tinted with sediment. A megachurch's illuminated cross, as tall as the mast of a great ship, rolls over the horizon. My son says, "The fear stems from how the heavy makeup conceals and exaggerates the wearer's face. Also, the bulbous nose."

"Do ballerinas carry a lot of clout in Russia?" I ask.

"It's like being a football player in Texas. Like being one of the Cowboys."

"Hot damn," I say because it sometimes gets a laugh. Not tonight. He's too wound up; he's been x-ing out days on his calendar for two months. "Are we talking Landry years or Johnson years?"

"Landry. No question."

That Asher knows his Dallas Cowboys history always calms me. I'm suddenly more comfortable in the truck's cab. My wedding band catches the light of the low moon, reminding me of thrown copper. I say, "A lot of wide receivers study ballet. It helps with spatial awareness."

"Besides Santa Claus," Asher says, "Ronald McDonald is the most recognized figure in the world."

At the hotel, two giant plywood clown faces command the lobby. From chin to crown, they're eight feet tall. Asher stands in front of them while I check in—he's so enthralled that I half expect him to kneel—and only moves when a long-haired woman asks him to snap pictures of her posing between the clowns. The desk clerk hands me breakfast coupons and keycards, Asher's welcome packet and lanyard. Our room's on the sixth floor. As we ascend in a glass elevator, Asher tells me the long-haired woman has been here a week and she estimates there are over a hundred clowns at the hotel. "Tough luck for coulrophobics," I say, and he smiles like I've passed an exam. It fills my every cell with breath. My mystifying son—the boy can send a tight, arcing spiral forty yards, but he'd rather hole up in his room with Red Skelton videos. After showering, he emerges from the bathroom wearing a shirt that reads *Can't Sleep, Clowns Will Eat Me* and orders room service. Throughout the night, the hotel trembles when the nearby planes take off. I wake up often, confused as to how we got where we are.

I work in oil and gas. I'm a geological technician, which means I spend my days pulling well information. I study maps generated by geologists and run numbers to track which wells are still producing and which need to be plugged and abandoned. I like knowing what's burning beneath our feet, the black oil and farther down, the clean effervescing gas. The knowledge makes me feel simultaneously large and small, and in that I find comfort. After I blew out my knee during a college scrimmage, I switched my major from communications to geology. I wanted, I think, to encase myself in rock, in hard things that last.

Geo techs don't make a lot of money; we leave that to engineers and landmen. This trip to Houston is a stretch, and although I could've saved half a month's pay by booking a room in the motor court across the freeway, I didn't want to skimp on what Asher's taken to calling the most important weekend of his "career." I want him to feel fussed over. I want him to know I'm on his team. As the convention approached, I imagined moments we might share: father and son splitting their first can of Lone Star, talking about the birds and bees, or maybe passing the pigskin, analyzing the pitiful seasons the Cowboys have been suffering, the injuries and heartbreaks that now define a once-great team. (Before we left Corpus, I aired up our old football and dropped it into the truck bed, just in case.) I also thought it might be a chance for us to finally talk about his mother. Jill's been gone two years. She was forty, and the first time she visited the doctor, the tumors lit her X-rays like a distant constellation. Three months later, the images were blurred with metastases. "Like a snowstorm," Jill said, sounding oddly pleased. She didn't make it to Thanksgiving. Asher and I avoided turkey that year and ordered pizza, then we went to a movie full of explosions and rooftop chases. "We'll make new traditions," I said. That Christmas he asked for his first makeup kit and a foam nose.

On Saturday morning, at the breakfast buffet, I realize my son will likely get thumped in his contest. He's just outmatched. Even with their painted faces, these clowns look severe and cagey. Purposeful, I think. Ornery. There are probably thirty of them in the restaurant, and another fifty mingling in the atrium. Their costumes are elaborate and expensive—billowy and silken and intensely colored. Pigment assaults me. They wear patent leather shoes as big as rural mailboxes. Two of them walk on stilts and can rest their elbows atop the plywood clown heads in the lobby. Some are bald. Others are neon geysers of hair—red and orange and purple, Afroed and spiky and twisted into formidable braids. One clown wears goggles and flippers and a small inflated pool around her waist. They're all adults, I'd guess mostly in their sixties, and they've come from as far away as Quebec and Maine. Seriousness radiates from them like heat from asphalt. They have swagger and business cards.

I'm embarrassingly relieved Asher didn't come to breakfast. He's awake but wanted to rehearse his routine alone in the room. His event is Paradeability. He'll be judged on the originality of his act and how many times he can complete it while moving through a gauntlet of would-be parade spectators. We've practiced in our backyard with a stopwatch. We record the sessions with a video camera propped on our propane grill, then Asher studies the footage and makes adjustments. As I eat my omelet, I catch myself hoping they give out ribbons for participation, something he can at least hang on his wall.

A clown in the hotel atrium starts squeezing a bicycle horn while another skips in circles, tossing confetti. His limberness surprises me. In a high falsetto, they sing, "We're having a hoot, an absolute hoot!" It's easy to imagine Jill here, trailing Asher, snapping candid pictures of him with the clowns. At home, framed photos of him hang on almost every wall—Asher selling raffle tickets, Asher feeding a brown pelican on Padre Island, Asher sleeping. Photography wasn't her hobby—watching Asher was. She was rarely in front of the camera, something I realized too late. Her absence blitzes me everywhere. The way the sheet and pillows on her side of the bed stay undisturbed, regardless of how I toss in my sleep, is menacing. The junk mail that still comes addressed to her leaves me as cored out as a cantaloupe. Lately, on Sunday mornings,

I've been hitting open houses in different neighborhoods in Corpus, trying to wrap my head around moving. I tell Asher I'm going to church. Maybe he believes me.

"Here's someone who knows *eggs*-actly what he likes for breakfast," a woman says. She's beside my booth, but a beat passes before I realize she's talking to me. She's in a pinstripe suit, wielding a clipboard and walkie-talkie.

"Do what?" I say.

"Professor Sparkles got me with that one earlier this morning, but when I say it, people just seem baffled," she says. She extends her hand. "I'm Dayna. With a *y*."

"I'm—"

"Asher's daddy," she says.

I shake her hand, puzzled, wondering what kind of information is on that clipboard. Then I remember her: the woman from last night, the one Asher visited with while I registered. Her hair is up this morning, and she looks like a pretty librarian, drab amongst all the color. I say, "Are you a clown parent, too?"

"I wish," she says. "Mine's a cheerleader. She'd walk five miles to avoid a clown."

"I suspect that may be an epidemic among cheerleaders."

"Asher's a cutie. What kind of clown is he?"

"Hobo," I say.

"I would've guessed auguste."

"He likes thrift stores," I say.

"An original, I love it. Come to enough of these and you see the same getups every year."

"This is our first. I'm afraid we're out of our league."

"Horsefeathers," Dayna says. "You're *eggs*-actly where you're supposed to be."

I smile and take a sip of cold coffee. "Professor Sparkles would give you high marks for that one."

"Let's hope not. Last time a clown left marks on me, my husband almost put both of us through a window."

Behind Dayna two clowns are covering a conference room door with pink balloons. Because I can't think of how to respond, I say, "That's not so good."

"Fourth floor, the Hilton in Nashville. Three years ago."

"I didn't know clowns were so prone to scandal."

"Neither did I," she says. "Isn't it fun?"

His name is Po' Boy the Hoboy. He keeps a notebook with ideas for costumes and gags, and on the cover, in pillowy letters, he's written, *Pretty Much the Only Property of Po' Boy the Hoboy*. He subscribes to a quarterly called *Clown Alley*. He's saving for a unicycle. Every couple of weeks we make thrift store rounds, hoping to scare up plaid trousers and polka-dot bow ties. Once, he found a dented bowler hat at the Salvation Army and cradled it like a wounded animal the whole drive home. He spends hours in the bathroom applying and reapplying his slap. I'm positive he's never kissed a girl.

Not that he'd make a bad catch. He has his mother's eyes and dark hair. A good jaw and nice posture, sturdy shoulders. Before he cottoned to clowning, I had him pegged as a quarterback, maybe scholarship material. He used to love watching the Cowboys and casting for redfish in Baffin Bay. His grades are good, but not so good that he eats lunch alone; any chance he gets, he incorporates clowns into school projects. He has friends, kids who call too late at night, who invite him to the beach. Last year he flirted with cigarettes for a month; his clothes smelled of sour smoke when I did the wash, but just when I gathered the nerve to confront him, the odor evaporated. Occasionally he'll get detention for cutting up or skipping algebra, and I admit those infractions probably leave me feeling the way other parents do when their kids make honor roll. I'll manufacture some annoyed concern and tell him to mow the yard as punishment, but really it's in those moments when I feel most like a father, when my blood duty is clearly defined, when I halfway believe I can do right by my inscrutable son.

After breakfast, I find him in front of the mirror in our room, adjusting his red foam nose. He's painted on a charcoal beard, and his cheeks and eyes are chalky. His eyebrows are thick rectangles. He wears his bowler and baggy pants, a necktie as wide as a flounder and two-tone bowling shoes. I suspect the shoes are stolen. They appeared two weeks ago, after he went to a bowling birthday party.

"Looking mighty fine," I say. I've brought up pastries and chocolate milk that I show him in the mirror.

"I had my bow tie on, but I looked butler-ish."

"Good call," I say. "It's a sea of bow ties down there. Originality matters."

Asher studies his reflection. He's remote again, the giddiness from last night buried under his slap. I wouldn't mind starting to chip away at his hopes for tomorrow's contest, but I can't figure out how, so I just sit on my bed and watch him. He fiddles with his tie, loosening and tightening, then moves toward the pastries. He shakes the milk carton and debates between a muffin and Danish. His mother used to do this. She never knew what she'd order until the last moment, and then it was even odds whether she'd flag the waiter and reverse her decision. He opts for the Danish.

"I didn't see any other hobos this morning," I say, though I'm not sure that's true.

He chews, takes a swig of milk. In the too-big clothes, he appears younger than he is. He says, "The hardcore clowns will come tomorrow for the contests. Today's novice-y. There's a talk on balloon sculpting. Workshops on improv and face-painting."

"Hot damn," I say. "Should I bring the video camera?"

"I think you'd need a conference badge."

"I bet there's an auguste who'd look the other way for a few jars of face cream."

Asher puts his Danish on the dresser. He slips into his blazer. There are mismatched patches sewn randomly on the coat; I stitched them using a needle and thread from Jill's nightstand. He says, "I just don't want you to be bored."

I'm about to say that whatever we do will be fine, I only want to spend the day by his side, but then I realize he's brushing me off. My mouth goes thick. I'm awash in a blunted, disconnected feeling, like I'm nothing more than a family friend watching someone else's kid for the weekend. I resist an urge to ask where he got his bowling shoes.

"Sure thing," I say. "I need to review some maps anyway, run some petroleum numbers."

He pulls a pair of fingerless gloves from his pocket and tugs them on. He says, "Are you going to church tomorrow?"

Maybe there's an edge of suspicion in his tone, maybe not. Either way, my guard goes up. At last week's open house, the realtor glanced at my wedding ring and suggested arranging a time to show my wife the property. I gave her a false name and the phone number for La Cocina, a Mexican place where Asher and I used to get takeout. Now I say, "I'd planned on skipping. I feel a bout of heresy coming on."

He steps back from the mirror, assessing his costume. My heart goes panicky. I'm afraid he's about to call me out on church or ban me from watching him compete tomorrow, but instead he says, "Then we should practice in the morning."

"I was thinking," I say, "if you'd rather just watch tomorrow, maybe get ideas for next year, I'd be game. We can make this an annual trip."

"It's in Chicago next year."

"One of America's finest cities," I say, though I've never been. "We'll make a vacation of it."

"Sweet," he says. "If I win tomorrow, next year's fees are waived. They want you to defend your title."

"The most important thing is to enjoy yourself," I say.

He crosses back to the dresser, takes another drink of milk. I think he's about to reach for his Danish again, but he goes for the muffin. He tears off a piece with his fingers and places it in his mouth like a dip of snuff. He chews slowly, careful not to disturb his makeup.

Before Asher goes downstairs, I take pictures of him on our balcony. He acts put upon, but he enjoys posing. We make plans to eat dinner together—it's clear he agrees to this out of pity, but I'm elated nonetheless—and then he's gone. In his wake, the room is littered with makeup sponges and a silence so complete I have to turn on the television. I surf the channels, flipping past adult pay-per-view, public access preachers, and movies with actors I don't recognize. I exhaust the stations a second time, then a third. I try to review the maps for the new prospect my office is vying for, an oil play down near Laredo, but my thoughts keep veering. I worry that losing the contest will undo Asher. I worry that for all the ways I know I'm letting him down—my inability to buy the toothpaste and fabric softener he likes, the grief I occasionally allow him to glimpse, my lies about church, our eating too much takeout—there are still deeper, more insidious failures that will only rise to the surface after doing irreparable damage. It's disorienting, such melancholy. I can't remember a day when I haven't thought that, with his mother gone, I've forgotten how to be a father. Not a day when I haven't thought, I used to be good at this. I leave a note—addressed to Po' Boy rather than Asher—saying I'll be in the hotel bar.

The bar is closed, though, and the lobby is mostly deserted. A family is checking out while a housekeeper, a woman with multiple earrings, polishes the granite planters by the elevator. Behind closed conference room doors, I hear the murmur of people speaking into podium microphones. "Obviously," a man says, "miming wouldn't work there. You have to use your noodle." The plywood clown faces have been commandeered as message centers. There are pamphlets for a San Antonio clown camp tacked to a cheek, a sign-up sheet for ride-share on a nose, and pieces of personal correspondence all over—

folded notes addressed to Spangles the Clown, Purple Peggy, Sir Smile-A-Lot. A table next to the door covered in pink balloons serves as a lost and found. So far, the only thing that's been lost is a yellow feather boa. The door is propped open with a box holding a disco ball. No lights are burning in the room, so the surfaces are dim, given to deep shadow. Most everything is draped in sheets.

Then a switch is flipped and fluorescent light opens the space. It's the vendors' area. A man in denim shorts and rainbow suspenders emerges from the back, whipping sheets from the tables. He says, "When you see something you can't live without, just holler."

The vendors' area is an L-shaped corridor; it might normally be a hallway leading to the laundry room or kitchen. Inside, I feel the inexplicable need to move stealthily. There are displays of leather shoes—jester-toed and oblong, sequined and high-heeled—and a few tables boasting nothing but makeup. There's a walk-in booth with frilly costumes on hangers and an elaborate wig arrangement—thirty Styrofoam heads, tiered according to style. Tables are devoted to magic tricks, juggling props, and party favors. The suspendered man leafs through a convention program in an airbrushing booth. He's surrounded by wispy clown portraits and stacks of white T-shirts emblazoned with his handiwork. At the far end of the corridor is an open space with a rack of unicycles and large three-wheeled bikes. I pick up a chrome unicycle, as if gauging its weight, though I have no idea how to assess such a strange machine. I lift it to my shoulder like a rifle and sight down the frame, foolishly making sure it's straight.

"Careful," the man says, "she's loaded."

I lower the tire to the ground, bounce it a couple of times to check the pressure. "How much?"

"That's Zany Laney's booth. She'll be back after the balloon talk."

I wheel the unicycle back to the rack.

"What type of clown are you?" he asks, bored.

Without thinking, I say, "Hobo."

"Hobos are destitute. Where's he getting the scratch for a unicycle?"

"I'm mixing it up. Come to enough of these and you see the same things over and over."

The man shrugs, puts his program under his chair, then goes to straighten the pallets of airbrushed shirts on his table. He says, "I like hobos. Emmett Kelly, Otto Griebling. It's the only truly American clown."

"You ever get folks asking you to airbrush their faces on goose eggs?"

"Son," he says, "I've been asked to airbrush faces on things that haunt my dreams."

"How long does it take?"

"To haunt my dreams?"

"To airbrush a face on something."

"Depends on the face. Depends on the something."

I like the suspendered man, his irascibility. I like how he's unfolding the shirts and then gingerly refolding them so his artwork is more visible. He's the size of a nose tackle. I say, "I'm not actually a clown."

"And thus the mystery of the unicycling hobo is solved."

"My son is, though. I'd like to get his face painted on something."

"Regrettably, I believe the gift shop is fresh out of goose eggs."

"How long will you be here?" I ask.

"Until the Lord our God rises again or happy hour, whichever comes first."

In the lobby, there are huddles of clowns deciding which workshops to attend. Someone, somewhere, puffs at a kazoo. Dayna is sitting with an auguste, an unhinged-looking woman in her seventies, and speaking into her walkie-talkie. I don't see Asher. Another hobo has materialized, though, a hunched man shuffling around with a sign that reads CAN YOU SPARE A LAUGH? I watch him, searching out anything that might prove useful for Asher, but the hobo just mopes by, wearing a hangdog expression and tuxedo pants cut off at the calves. One clown waves him away, but another grants him a belly laugh; it's showy and territorial. The hobo bows. Then he catches sight of a clown with a tinselly wig pushing a whiteface in a wheelchair, and he's all energy as he maneuvers in front of them. They stop, and he brandishes his sign with a cocked head, pleading. The man in the wheelchair nods. He hunts around for something in his lap. I think he's misread the sign and is looking for change, but then he produces a device, one of those mechanical larynx numbers, and presses it to his throat. I don't hear anything at first, but soon there are low peals of disembodied laughter vibrating toward me like a flock of harsh, metallic birds. I retreat into the parking lot, the sad noise still buzzing in my ears when I reach my truck.

. . .

Hobo clowns likely came out of the Great Depression, though it's possible their roots stretch back to vaudeville. Asher wrote a report for his history class. They're forlorn and downtrodden, ever the brunt of jokes. They're always on the receiving end of pies to the face, kicks to the keister. That Asher reinvented himself as the only clown without hope or mirth bothers me. I assume it's because of his mother, but maybe not. I'm afraid to ask.

And yet when he returns to the room on Saturday evening, he's jazzed up and garrulous. I'm immediately optimistic about dinner. Maybe we'll split that beer. Maybe I'll find words to inoculate him against tomorrow's disappointment. He hangs his blazer on the desk chair and tells me, breathlessly, about the compliments he's gotten on his costume, about learning to twist balloons into airplanes and dinosaurs. Better still, a workshop instructor said he had such a knack for painting faces that he could get work at birthday parties. The instructor suggested setting up a website, running classified ads in the paper, acquiring a tax ID number.

He's in front of the mirror again. I think he's wiping off his makeup, but soon realize he's touching it up. I say, "Will Po' Boy be joining us for dinner?"

"Change of plans," he says. "The Calliope Ball is tonight. It's unmissable."

"You have to eat, Ash."

"There's a buffet. Mexican, I think. We can eat down there."

"We? What happened to that airtight clown security?"

"I scored you a badge from Mrs. Barrett," he says. "She didn't want you feeling left out."

"Mrs. Barrett?"

In the mirror, I can see him clipping on a bow tie, sliding the stem of a plastic sunflower through a hole in his lapel. Outside, a jet is descending and the noise rattles the windows.

"Ash?" I say.

"You met her at breakfast."

"Dayna?"

"She's the director of the conference. She said you seemed lonesome."

The lobby is transformed by darkness and oldies music. The disco ball I saw earlier now hangs from a tapestry of Christmas lights, spinning and refracting color. Asher hands me my badge and says he'll meet me in the room later, then, before I can protest, he squeezes into the crowd and disappears. Clowns sidle past each other with plates of enchiladas raised above their heads. I smell chili powder and corn tortillas. The suspendered man is sipping a beer by the glass elevator, chatting with two clowns in tutus. When he sees me, he cocks his arm and pantomimes throwing a pass. Seconds later, I act like I've caught it, right in the numbers.

I climb the stairs to the second-floor balcony and peer down. Asher is already talking shop with the shuffling hobo and a female auguste. They're interested in whatever he's saying, nodding and letting him go on, and I hate that I didn't bring the camera. Jill would have. She would have stood beside me, snapping pictures and watching the mass of clowns move below us like a cloud of phosphorescent marsh gas. I try to imagine which costumes she'd like. It's a habit. When I take

Asher to the mall, I guess which necklaces she'd want from jewelry store windows. Driving to my open houses, I keep an eye out for gardens she'd appreciate, and inside the rooms, I envision how she'd arrange our furniture, where she'd hang the photos of Asher. Now, I wonder if she'd like the cowboy with the checkerboard Stetson and matching boots. The woman in the yellow jumper and platinum wig? The scarecrow with a black balloon raven perched on his shoulder? I feel no affinity for any of them. They all look grave and infirm to me, an endangered species, a well that will soon be dry and abandoned.

A female clown, a whiteface in a pink jester costume, walks onto the balcony. She wears a ruffled collar and a three-point hat. I assume she's looking for someone in the group below, but she steps closer and says, "Sulking alone wasn't quite what I intended when I gave Asher your badge."

"Dayna?"

"Call me Ginger," she says. "Ginger the Jester."

"I didn't know you were a clown," I say.

"I'm good with secrets."

The glass elevator, packed tight with whitefaces, passes the balcony and stops in the lobby. Asher is still with the hobo and auguste, and soon he's being introduced to someone in a skunk costume. He doffs his bowler. The skunk curtsies. I feel conspicuous with Dayna beside me. Maybe Asher wouldn't recognize her dressed as a jester, or maybe keeping tabs on his old man is the furthest thing from his mind, but I worry. Before Jill died, she'd joke about my romantic future. "One year's too soon," she'd say, "but if you're not ringing some gal's bell by year three, I will, from on high, assume you've switched teams."

I did an intentionally poor job of masking how much I despised such talk, but later, when she'd lost so much weight and asked me to promise that I'd eventually move on—"For me," she'd said, weeping, "for Ash"—I had conceded only to spare us the rest of the conversation. I can't remember the last time I stood this close to a woman. Dayna's perfume smells of daylilies. Her gloves are satin. My blood is teeming with a miserable, traitorous vitality.

Dayna has been talking. She says, "That's what my daughter calls it, the John Wayne Gacy Convention."

"Asher wanted to do a school project on him, but I banned it. I got the silent treatment for a week," I say. I'd forgotten about that uncomfortable phase last year, when Asher was preoccupied with Gacy and seemed to always be spouting dark trivia. Gacy was a whiteface named Pogo. He painted sharp corners on his mouth, whereas traditional, non-mass-murdering clowns use round borders to keep from scaring children.

In the lobby, Asher is waving to a group in the glass elevator. They wave back as they ascend, the glimmer of the disco ball reflecting on the windowed wall. "Chantilly Lace" starts up. My heart feels dizzy in my chest.

"Kids are the pits," Dayna says, dancing a little with her bottom half. Behind her, the elevator opens and clowns slowly exit, like their joints hurt. Dayna says, "My daughter was spatting with another cheerleader, something about a boy, and she mixed Nair into the girl's shampoo. Can you say, 'suspension'? Can you say, 'permanent record'? Can you say—"

"How good?" I interrupt.

"I'm sorry?"

"You said you were good with secrets. How good?"

"Oh," she says, a lovely lilt in her tone, her hips still keeping time with the music. "Really good. Unfathomably good. Better than—"

"Room 618," I say.

"Wow," she says. "Okay. Wow."

"Take the stairs," I say, making for the elevator.

When I go to my open houses on Sunday mornings, I worry Asher thinks I'm meeting a woman. I expect to return home and find him waiting, his eyes narrow with betrayal. Asher at the kitchen table, glowering. Asher pacing the house and brooding over the questions he'll hurl at me like stones: Who is she? Do you love her? What would Mom think? But he's always asleep when I get back, the door to his room unopened since the night before. The house is disappointingly quiet, indicting in its stillness, so I wash the week's dishes to bide time until my son emerges. Sometimes I intentionally clang pots and pans together, then apologize for waking him. Had I not started telling him I was going to church, he wouldn't even know I'd been gone.

At the showings, I ask about school districts and property taxes, mortgage liens and mineral rights. Such questions, I think, paint me as a serious buyer, but I'm also hoping for some combination of answers that will spur me to action. Early on, I expected to be easily swayed. The smell of fresh paint and carpet, the gleam of marble counters and the pulsing sound of sprinkler systems in lush lawns—I thought they would prove irresistible and I'd want to make an offer on every property. But the houses punish me with newness, and I feel negligent and untethered, guilty for having left Asher at home. I can't actually imagine putting our house on the market or packing up our rooms. Once, the notion of surrendering my keys to another family brought me to tears. I was scrubbing bowls in the sink after visiting a three-bedroom ranch on Riley Drive, and Asher came out of his room and caught me.

"Dad, I think you're crying," he said, as if alerting me to a nosebleed. He wore his *Clowns Will Eat Me* shirt, his dark hair was mashed from the hard sleep of youth, and he seemed mortified to find me in such a state.

"The service this morning," I said. "It was beautiful."

On Sunday, the lobby has been transformed again for the Paradeability event. It's roped off in a zigzag course. One of the giant plywood faces marks the start point, the other stands at the finish line, and the route is lined with clowns and bleary-eyed family members slurping coffee. There are twice as many clowns as yesterday; if I look in one direction too long, the clashing colors make me lightheaded. I position myself halfway through the course and actually feel like I'm at a parade. Asher waits in queue with the other competitors, pacing. I worry he'll vomit or faint. He didn't return to the room until after one this morning, and although Dayna was long gone, it's possible he spied her leaving. When we practiced his routine before breakfast, he was off his game, sluggish and tentative, and his lassitude felt like an accusation.

Before each competitor enters the circuit, an announcer

rallies the crowd. He calls us *ladies and germs, fillies and foals, boys and girls*. If the clown is new to the competition, he says, "Ladies and germs, our next contestant is a First of May." But the event is sleepy, tedious. I have to keep turning the video camera back on because it times out between competitors. Some clowns juggle through the course—rings, bowling pins, rubber chickens. Others just mosey along cracking jokes. There's a hobo who sneezes into a paper sack every few steps and sends a plume of powder into the air, then he offers the contents of the bag to the crowd and mocks offense when we decline. The woman wearing flippers and the inflatable pool acts like she's swimming by, and every so often she spits a high arc of water into the audience. How she refills her mouth is a mystery. A whiteface in a silver astronaut costume stomps along, occasionally lifting her bubble helmet to shout, *Moonwalk!* There's a clown on stilts who moves in slow motion, reciting poetry with an Irish accent. Passing me, he says, "I, through the terrible novelty of light, stalk on, stalk on."

Then the announcer says, "Boys and girls, how's about another First of May?"

There's a smattering of applause, a long, bending whistle.

"Well then, ladies and germs, set my head on fire and put it out with a hammer, here's Po' Boy the Hoboy!"

For his routine, Asher wears a pair of boxing gloves and has a small cardboard box tied to his ankle with a yard-long cut of twine. Once the clock starts, he says, "You want a piece of me? I'm the best kickboxer you'll ever see!" Then he kicks the cardboard box ahead of him and starts bobbing and weaving and punching his way forward until he catches up to it again. Repeat, repeat, repeat. When he's throwing his jabs, he exhales through his red foam nose, sharp like a real pugilist. That was my idea. Granting the twine doesn't get tangled around his shoe, he can usually run through the routine six times in a minute.

And despite his lousy practice earlier, in the contest he's a crackerjack. I'm caught off guard by how his voice carries, the snap of his jab, the accuracy of his kick. The box lands directly in his path every time. When he passes, spectators whoop and cheer and sound horns. I feel like I'm in the bleachers at a bowl game and the audience wave is approaching. People maneuver for a better view; they lean and jostle and nod venerably. I record everything. I feel an almost unbearable pride, and my stomach roils with guilt for having ever doubted him. On his fourth stop, he's close enough that I have to unzoom the camera lens. "You want a piece of me?" he says to an auguste. She raises her hands in surrender. Everyone laughs.

Then, when he kicks the box, the twine breaks. The box is borne aloft, cartwheeling through the air, until, after what seems like minutes, it lands in the crowd. There's a collective gasping—"Holy smokes," someone says—and confusion as to whether this is part of Po' Boy's routine, a premeditated flourish at the end. Had he noticed the audience's credulity, Asher might've been able to call an audible. But he freezes. There's a wretched silence, and I want to run to him, to gather my son in my arms and spirit him away. By the time the box is being passed back toward him, he's composed enough to start throwing jabs again and proceed forward. I expect him to stop when he reaches the finish line, maybe to find me in the crowd so I can reassure or console him, but he bolts from the course. Everyone applauds, more confused than ever, while Asher heads for the exit. I stop recording just before he opens the door and disappears into the radiant sun. Then I go to our room.

Some mornings I wake up forgetting Jill is gone, and for a perfect crushing moment, a moment that is both too long and too brief, I think to reach for her in bed. Then I remember, and the old life recedes, like a tide being drawn back into the ocean. For the rest of the day, I feel halved. Other mornings, I'm positive I've lost Asher. Once, the fear was so consuming I snuck into his room and watched the blanket—a clown print—rise and fall with his breath; it was all I could do not to lie down beside him. Or I'll come home after work, calling his name as I close the front door, and if he doesn't answer right away, my heart will stutter. How often have I braced myself against finding a note, written in the same bubbly hand as Po' Boy's notebook, saying he's decided to light out on his own? I worry my son will run off with the circus the way parents of promiscuous daughters worry about abortions. I can't believe I'm enough to keep him here.

When I find Asher in the parking lot, he's on the tailgate of our truck, smoking a cigarette. In his costume and slap, and with the smoke ribboning into his eyes, he looks old and grizzled, convincingly penniless.

"Heads-up," I call from across the parking lot and wing our football toward him. I've had it in our room since yesterday and went to retrieve it after he fled the lobby. My pass is wobbly, shamefully so, but with his cigarette clamped between his lips, Asher scrambles and catches it.

"What's this?" he says, turning the ball over in his hands.

"It's you," I say.

It took the suspendered man only half an hour to cover the football with Po' Boy's image—charcoal beard, thick eyebrows, alabaster complexion, and crimson nose. He worked from the screen of our camera, using a picture I'd snapped of Asher that morning. The ball looked so fine, so astoundingly lifelike, I'd thought to hold on to it for a birthday or Christmas present—I never know what to buy—but I knew I wouldn't be able to wait. When I showed it to Dayna last night, she said, "You're a good father."

"My wife died," I said.

"Oh, sugar," she said, "I know that."

Maybe Asher told her. Maybe, given the hours she's spent surrounded by elaborate masks, my unpainted face seemed impossibly readable to her. I don't know. I broke into a humiliated sweat, sacked by guilt and relief, and willed Dayna to leave. Soon she kissed my scalp and slipped from the room without a word.

In the parking lot, Asher toes out his cigarette with his bowling shoe and blows a stream of smoke over his shoulder. The air smells acrid, poisoned. He studies the ball like a man deciding on a bottle of wine. He says, "This is pretty sweet, Dad."

"The gift shop was out of goose eggs," I say. Maybe he smiles a furtive smile, I can't tell. A silver jet rumbles into the sky behind him.

"The twine broke," he says.

"There should've been a flag on the play."

"It's never happened before."

"You handled it like a pro," I say. "Next time we'll use a nylon cord."

He spins the ball in the air, catches it. He says, "I don't smoke a lot. I just bummed that cigarette from a housekeeper coming off her break. I'm sorry."

I avert my eyes, arrange a pensive expression on my face. He expects me to be angry, and I know I should be. I should ground him. I should ask if he's taken a good gander at that crippled clown with the mechanical larynx. I'm aware of this just as I'm aware of the oil and gas coursing miles beneath our feet. This is prime fathering time here, the moment when I should impart solid, inviolable wisdom that will serve as his north star and guide him into a healthy future. But right now every truth seems porous, every judgment skewed. I feel something give inside my chest, as surely as when my knee buckled in the scrimmage and I knew my world was forever altered. When I look at Asher—the dour mask, the clothes that once belonged to someone else, the weary secrets buried beneath his obsession—I see only the smallest traces of the boy Jill and I raised together. Instead, I see myself. It gives me vertigo, this recognition, like I'm staring at a mirror that I've always taken for a window.

Asher is looking at his football again. I think he likes it, but I'm careful not to betray how much this pleases me. Cars and trucks are swooshing by on the freeway. A plane is about to touch down.

Asher says, "I really am sorry about smok—"

"Come to church with me," I interrupt.

"Right now?"

"Next week," I say. "I think a little fellowship might be in order."

He nods, contrite. He thinks I mean to scold him, and I'll let that ride to keep him honest, but punishment never enters my mind. The prospect of our finding a church together is invigorating, and I feel as though we're on the verge of something essential forming between us. We'll get dressed up. We'll file into a holy building and take our places among men in bow ties and old women with powdered cheeks and bright lips, believers seeking shelter. We'll sing and pray, confess our sins and mourn our dead. We'll kneel before ancient altars, behold the glory of ritual and sacrifice. We'll weep and be saved. We'll go every Sunday. After services, Asher and I will hit a thrift store, or we'll swing by an open house and try to divine the years ahead. We'll talk about girls and college and his mother. We'll talk until our voices grow hoarse. When we return home, I'll slap a couple of steaks on the grill and we'll scroll through TV channels, looking for a game. If the Cowboys are playing, the stands will be packed with fragile men wearing wild wigs and oversized jerseys and war paint on their faces. Asher and I will root for all of them, the heartsick fans and their doomed, beleaguered team. We'll hold our breath when the quarterback lets fly with a Hail Mary. We'll hope for a miracle as the receiver stumbles toward the end zone. His arms will be extended and his legs weak and his palms open to the sky, and from where we sit, from our house, he'll look like a man trying to outrun everything behind him, like a man begging, at last, for mercy.

ENCOUNTERS WITH UNEXPECTED ANIMALS

Lambright had surprised everyone by offering to drive his son's girlfriend home. The girl was three months shy of seventeen, two years older than Robbie. She'd been held back in school. Her driver's license was currently suspended. She had a reputation, a body, and a barcode tattooed on the back of her neck. Lambright sometimes glimpsed it when her green hair was ponytailed. She'd come over for supper this evening, and though she volunteered to help Robbie and his mother with the dishes, Lambright had said he'd best deliver her home, it being a school night. He knew this pleased his wife and Robbie, the notion of him giving the girl another chance.

Driving, Lambright thought the moon looked like a fingerprint of chalk. They headed south on Airline Road. A couple of miles and he'd turn right on Saratoga, then left onto Everhart, and eventually they'd enter Kings Crossing, the subdivision with pools and sprinkler systems. At supper, Robbie and the girl had told, in tandem, a story about playing hide-and-seek on the abandoned country club golf course. Hide-and-seek, Lambright thought, is that what y'all call it now? Then the conversation moved to encounters with unexpected animals. The girl had once seen a blue and gold macaw riding on the headrest of a man's passenger seat, and another time, in a pasture in the Rio Grande Valley, she'd spotted zebras grazing among cattle. Robbie's mother recalled finding goats in the tops of peach trees in her youth. Robbie told the story of visiting the strange neighborhood in San Antonio where the muster of peacocks lived, and it led the girl to confess her desire to get a fan of peacock feathers tattooed on her lower back. She also wanted a tattoo of a busted magnifying glass hovering over the words *Fix Me*.

Lambright couldn't figure what she saw in his son. Until the girl started visiting, Robbie had superhero posters on his walls and a fleet of model airplanes suspended from the ceiling with fishing wire. Lambright had actually long been skeptical of the boy's room, worrying it looked too childish, worrying it confirmed some softness of character. But now the walls were stripped and all that remained of the fighter fleet was the fishing-wire stubble on the ceiling, and he understood he'd never really been all that concerned. Two weeks ago, one of his wife's necklaces disappeared. Last week, a bottle of her nerve pills. Then, over the weekend, he'd caught Robbie and the girl with a flask of whiskey in the backyard. She'd come to supper tonight to make amends.

Traffic was light. When he stopped at the intersection of Airline and Saratoga, the only headlights he saw were far off, like buoys in the bay. The turn signal dinged. He debated, then clicked it off. He accelerated straight across Saratoga.

"Mr. Lambright? We were supposed to turn—"

"Scenic route," he said. "We'll visit a little."

But they didn't. There was only the low hum of the tires on

the road, the noise of the truck pushing against the wind. Lambright hadn't contributed anything to the animal discussion earlier, but now he considered mentioning what he'd read a while back, how bald eagle nests are often girded with cat collars, strung with the little bells and tags of lost pets. He stayed quiet, though. They were out near the horse stables now. The air smelled of alfalfa and manure. The streetlights had fallen away.

The girl said, "I didn't know you could get to Kings Crossing like this."

They crossed the narrow bridge over Oso Creek, then came into a clearing, a swath of clay and patchy brush, gnarled mesquite trees.

"Mr. Lambright, my parents might be getting worried. Like you said, it being a school night."

He pulled onto the road's shoulder. Caliche pinged against the truck's chassis. He dowsed his headlights, and the scrub around them silvered, turned to moonscape. They were outside the city limits, miles from where the girl lived. He killed the engine.

"Mr. Lambright," she said, "I know you have doubts about me. I know I'm not—"

"Cut him loose," Lambright said.

"Do what?"

"Give it a week, then tell him you've got someone else."

Her eyes scanned the night through the windshield. Maybe she was getting her bearings, calculating how far out they were. Cows lowed somewhere in the darkness. She said, "Mr. Lambright, I love Rob—"

"You're a pretty girl. You've been to the rodeo a few times. You'll do all right. But not with him."

The chalky moon was in and out of clouds. A wind buffeted the truck and kicked up the odor of the brackish creek. The girl was picking at her cuticles, which made her look docile.

"Is there anything I can say here? Is there something you're wanting to hear?"

"You can say you'll quit him," Lambright said. "I'd like to have your word on that subject."

"And if I don't, you'll leave me on the side of the road?"

"We're just talking. We're sorting out a problem."

"Or you'll beat me up and throw me in the creek?"

"You're too much for him. He's overmatched."

"And so if I don't dump him, you'll, what, rape me? Murder me? Bury me in the dunes?"

"Lizzie," he said, his tone pleasingly superior. He liked how much he sounded like a father.

Another wind blew, stiff and parched, rustling the trees. To Lambright, they appeared to shiver, like they'd gotten cold. A low cloud unspooled on the horizon. The cows were quiet.

"I see how you look at me, you know," she said, shifting toward him. She unbuckled her seatbelt, the noise startlingly loud in the truck. Lambright's eyes went to the rearview mirror: no one around. She scooted an inch closer. Two inches. Three. He smelled lavender, her hair or cool skin. She said, "Everyone sees it. Nobody'll be surprised you drove me out here."

"I'm telling you to stay away from my boy."

"In the middle of the night, in the middle of nowhere."

"There's no mystery here," Lambright said.

"Silly," she said.

"Do what?"

"I said you're silly. There's mystery all around us. Goats in trees. Macaws in cars."

Enough, Lambright thought. He cranked the ignition, switched on his headlights.

"A man who drives his son's underage girl into remote areas, that's awfully mysterious."

"Just turn him loose," he said.

"A girl who flees the truck and comes home dirty and crying. What will she tell her parents? Her boyfriend? The man's depressed wife?"

"Just leave him be," he said. "That's the takeaway tonight."

"Will the police be called? Will they match the clay on her shoes to his tires?"

"Lizzie—"

"Or will she keep it to herself? Will it be something she and the man always remember when they see each other? When she marries his son, when she bears his grandbabies? These are bona fide mysteries, Mr. Lambright."

"Lizzie," he said. "Lizzie, let's be clear."

But she was already out of the truck, sprinting toward the creek. She flashed through the brush and descended the bank, and Lambright was shocked by the languid swiftness with which she crossed the earth. Blood was surging in his veins, like he'd swerved to miss something in the road and his truck had just skidded to a stop and he didn't yet know if he was hurt, if the world was changed. The passenger door was open, the interior light burning, pooling. The girl jumped across the creek and bolted alongside it. She cut to and fro. He wanted to see her as an animal he'd managed to avoid, a rare and dangerous creature he'd describe for Robbie when he got home, but really her movement reminded him of a trickle of water tracking through pebbles. It stirred in him a floating sensation, the curious and scattered feeling of being borne on waves or air or wings. He was disoriented, short of breath. He knew he was at the beginning of something, though just then he couldn't say exactly what.

SOLDIER OF FORTUNE

Her name was Holly Hensley, and except for the two years when her father was transferred to a naval base in Florida, her family lived across the street from mine. This was on Beechwood Drive, in Corpus Christi, Texas. Our parents held garage sales together, threw hurricane parties, went floundering in the shallow, bottle-green water under the causeway. If the Hensleys were working overtime and Holly was staying late for pep squad practice—which meant grinding against Julio Chavez in the backseat of his Skylark—my mother would pick up Holly's younger brother from daycare and watch him until they got home. Sam had been born while they were living in Florida. ("My old man got one past the goalie," Holly liked to say. "There's nothing more disgusting.") In 1986, the year everything happened at the Hensley house, Sam was three. Holly was eighteen, a senior at King High School, and I was a freshman, awkward and shy and helpless with love.

Most mornings we walked to school together. Holly's hair would be wet from the shower, her eyes wide and glassy with fatigue; she'd yawn and say, "What's buzzin', cousin?" She liked to drag her fingers along the chain-link fences we passed, and to stop at Maverick Market to buy Diet Cokes and steal candy bars. I waited outside, worrying she'd get caught. We talked about what she'd do after graduation—some days she planned to enroll at the beauty college, others she wanted to dance at the Fox's Den out by the oil refineries—and about Roscoe, the collie she'd adopted in Florida. She told me how her little brother preferred her Aggie sweatshirt to his baby blanket. I invented stories of girls I'd been with, wild things named Rhonda and Anastasia who attended different schools and who, I hoped, might make Holly jealous. Usually, she'd just bump me with her hip and say, "You're more of a slut than I am." We never talked about the rumors that she and Julio had let a crowd of kids watch them in bed at a homecoming party or that she'd recently been spotted leaving the Sea Ranch motel with Mr. Mitchell, the geology teacher. Even my parents had heard about Mr. Mitchell. My mother said Holly was just trying to get her parents' attention, acting out because of the new baby. My father said she was trouble and if he caught me alone with her, he'd whip my ass. But I rarely saw her after we got to campus. Holly would disappear onto the school's smoking patio, a dismal slab of concrete where stringy-haired surfers and kids with safety pins through their eyebrows loitered, and I would go find Matt Rickard.

Matt and I had been friends since elementary. We'd played on the same soccer team, joined and quit Boy Scouts together, leaned despondently against the gym bleachers and watched couples sway at the junior high dances our parents made us attend. In our freshman year, Matt wore sleeveless shirts and tucked the cuffs of his camouflage pants into military boots; he had a pair of fatigues for every day of the week—desert camo, woodland and blue woodland, tigerstripe and black tigerstripe. For a while, we'd been into guerilla warfare. We bought *Soldier of Fortune* magazine, made blowguns from copper tubing, slathered our faces with mud when we crept under the lacey mesquite trees behind his house. We saved our allowances for the gun expos at the Memorial Coliseum and loaded up on Chinese throwing stars and bandoliers of blank bullets, butterfly knives and pamphlets on choke holds and MREs that tasted like glue. We ate meals with the forks and spoons attached to our Swiss Army knives. Over the summer, though, I'd grown bored and embarrassed by the warfare stuff—my walls had been draped with camouflage netting, and over my bed, I'd had a poster of one ninja roundhousing another—but Matt still liked it so I'd recently told him he could have my cache. He was disappointed in me, I knew, as if I'd defected to the enemy, and probably the reason he hadn't yet come to collect my stuff was the hope that I'd change my mind. But I'd already packed everything into my army duffel and each afternoon, I waited for Matt to take it away. I didn't think we'd stay friends much longer.

When my father came into my room on a Friday night in early October, I thought he'd say Matt was on the porch. I was on my bed, staring at the acoustic ceiling where the ninja poster had been and listening to my stereo. My father crossed the room and lowered the volume. He wore a short-sleeved shirt and a clip-on tie; he'd just gotten off work. He gazed through my window and into the backyard.

"Is Matt here?" I asked.

"You need to take care of Holly's dog for a few days."

"Roscoe," I said.

"Make sure he has food and water. Maybe play with him a little."

I sat up on my bed. My father's voice sounded frayed, as if I were hearing him from far away. His hands were clasped behind his back. I thought I smelled cigarette smoke on him, but then I realized it was floating down the hall from the kitchen.

"Are they heading out of town?" I asked. The Hensleys had a van and sometimes drove to the Hill Country.

"Don't go over there tonight," he said. "You can just start in the morning."

"Okay," I said. A wind gusted outside. Tallow branches scraped against the side of the house.

"If the dog shits on their patio, spray it down with the hose."

"Is Mom smoking again?"

"She might be, Josh," he said and put his hand against the window. "Yes, that might be happening."

In 1986, my father worked at the naval air station—most everyone's father did, including Holly's and Matt's—but he was also moonlighting at Sears, selling radial tires and car batteries, which he blamed on Reagan. It was the year the president denied trading arms for hostages in Iran and the space shuttle *Challenger* exploded and Halley's Comet scorched through the sky. It was the year I loved a reckless girl, the year being around my best friend made me lonely. It was the year my mother was working at the dry-cleaning plant and trying to quit smoking. I knew she occasionally snuck cigarettes—I'd seen her in the backyard on evenings when my father was at Sears—but she hadn't smoked in our house for months. On that night in October, when the filmy scent of smoke wafted into my room, I could only think that Holly's family was moving again. The last time her father had gotten news of his transfer, they were gone within a week.

But they weren't leaving. There'd been an accident earlier that day, something involving Sam, Holly's little brother. My father knew only that Sam had been taken away in an ambulance and the Hensleys would likely spend a few nights with him at the hospital. He relayed the information in a detached tone, as if summarizing a movie he didn't want me to watch. He'd moved from the window to sit on my bed, where he looked small. He said their mail would be held and there was a key under the ceramic cow skull on their porch. I tried to remember the last time I'd seen Sam, but couldn't—maybe the previous weekend, when he and Holly drew on their driveway with colored chalk, or maybe when Mr. Hensley was watering the yard with Sam on his shoulders. In my room, my father kept dragging his hand over his face, as if trying to wake himself up. I asked if he knew how Holly was doing, and he said, "She's hurting, Josh. They're all hurting like hell."

My mother baked all night—brownies and lemon bars, biscuits and an enchilada casserole. She fried chicken and sliced vegetables and made salami and cheese sandwiches that she quartered into triangles. When I came into the kitchen on Saturday morning, the counter was crowded with foil-covered dishes. My mother was walleyed. She poured me a glass of orange juice and put two pieces of cold fried chicken on my plate. "Breakfast of champions," she said.

With all the foil, the kitchen was bright and strange. The table was tacky with humidity. My mother shook a cigarette from a pack, then lit it from a burner on the stove. I heard it sizzle.

"Connie called last night," she said and exhaled smoke toward the ceiling. Connie was Mrs. Hensley, Holly's mother. My mother said, "Little Sam is sedated in intensive care."

"I don't know what's happening," I said.

"He burned himself," she said. "He's scalded all over the front of his little body."

Sam, my mother explained, had woken with a fever, so Mrs. Hensley kept him home from daycare. He spent the morning watching cartoons and napping on the living room couch. While he slept, Mrs. Hensley was cleaning the house and washing clothes, then decided to make tuna salad for lunch. She put water on to boil eggs. She checked on Sam on the couch, then stepped into the garage to put a load of laundry in the dryer. They had an attached garage, so she left the kitchen door open in case Sam woke up and called for her. She got sidetracked looking for dryer sheets and stayed out there longer than she'd intended. Then she heard her son screaming: He'd pulled the pot of boiling water down onto himself.

I pushed my plate away. At Sam's last birthday party, my parents and I had given him a toy garbage truck. Holly gave him a baseball cap that read *I Wasn't Born in Texas, But Got Here As Soon As I Could.* He'd been wearing it when Mr. Hensley watered their lawn.

My mother opened the oven, looked inside, and then closed the door. Her cigarette was in an ashtray on the counter, smoke climbing toward the open window.

"That poor family," my mother said.

"They're behind the eight ball," I said. It was a phrase my father used.

"They sure are," she said. "Connie couldn't find Holly until very late. She thought she was off with that Julio."

"She had pep squad practice," I lied. "I saw her when I walked home."

"You did?"

"There's a game this weekend," I said. "A big one."

"Then that's a relief. I worried she was with the teacher again."

"I don't think that really happened, the stuff with Mr. Mitchell," I said.

"I know you don't, sweetheart."

I took another bite of chicken, drained my orange juice. I said, "Matt might come over today. I'm giving him all my war stuff."

"I'll leave some chicken for you two," she said. "Your father and I are taking the rest to the hospital."

"I want to go," I said.

She brought her cigarette to her lips, then stubbed it out. She said, "No, Joshie, I don't think you do."

Their house had always been nicer than ours, and bigger. Over the years, workers had renovated the Hensleys' kitchen and added two rooms on the house's backside, a study and a game room. They had a bumper pool table, thick carpet and Saltillo tile, lights with dimmer switches, and a fireplace. "Who needs a fireplace in Corpus?" my father had said one night. He was squinting through the peephole in our front door, watching smoke rise from the Hensleys' chimney. "Don't try to be something you're not, boy," he told me, and then told me again when they bought an aboveground pool for their backyard right before Mr. Hensley was transferred to Florida. I'd assumed the transfer was a demotion or punishment, but my father said Hensley had applied for it. (By way of explanation, he'd only said, "They're Republicans, Joshie.") While they were away, the Hensleys rented the house to a Catholic deacon and his wife, and when they returned, they paid to have new vinyl siding installed. It was gray with white and black trim, the shades of a lithograph.

Until that October weekend, I'd never been alone in their house. It seemed illicit, like when Matt and I paged through his father's *Playboys*. The darkened rooms made me anxious. I had the sense I would do something I shouldn't, the dangerous and disappointing feeling that I couldn't be trusted. Had there been a route for me to bypass the house and still reach the garage where Roscoe's food was, I would've taken it, but I didn't have their garage door opener—their automatic door was another extravagance my father resented—so I had to cut through the kitchen. I went twice on Saturday, three times on Sunday. I moved like a thief on each visit, never lingering or touching what I didn't have to. The air in the house smelled of potpourri, cloistered and spiced, and I tried not to breathe. I averted my gaze from the familiar and mysterious artifacts of the Hensleys' lives.

And yet I couldn't keep from seeing the coffee table Mrs. Hensley had pulled over to the couch so Sam wouldn't roll off, Holly's Aggie sweatshirt spread over the cushions, little red high-top shoes upturned on the carpet. I pretended not to know the Hensleys and tried to piece together a different family based on evidence they'd left behind. *Their son is an only child,* I thought. *His parents have taken him to a swimming lesson.* Or I imagined all the Hensleys were home and hiding, waiting for me to break or steal something. My heart pumped in my ears. I left the lights off. In the kitchen, the floor tile gleamed; Holly's father had come home briefly Friday night to mop up the spilled water and grab fresh clothes for everyone at the hospital. The copper-bottomed pot was in the sink. Four unopened cans of tuna were stacked on the counter.

In the backyard, Roscoe always barreled into my legs and knocked me sideways. He jumped as high as my shoulders and scratched my chest through my shirt and licked my hand with his warm tongue. I let him chase me around the pool and I threw pine cones for him to catch. We wrestled in the grass the way Holly had said he liked, then I scratched the scruff of his neck until he snored. I fed him more than I should. Before school on Monday morning, maybe because I'd been hoping Holly would appear on her porch and we'd walk to school together, I opened one of the cans of tuna and let Roscoe eat it from a spoon. That evening there was diarrhea all over the patio.

At school, the story kept changing. Sam wasn't scalded, he'd drowned in the Hensleys' pool. He'd slipped on a wet floor and hit his head. His brain was swelling. He'd been hit by a car, he'd eaten roach poison. Someone claimed to have seen the geology teacher taking flowers to the hospital, and someone else said they'd been in the faculty parking lot and found him weeping in his station wagon. On Wednesday, Matt said he'd heard the whole thing was a lie to cover up how Sam had accidentally shot himself with his father's unregistered pistol.

We were standing by the statue of a mustang, the school mascot. Matt was in his blue woodland camos. He said, "I bet it was the Luger she showed us. If it was, the kid's toast."

Shortly after she'd returned from Florida, Holly had taken me and Matt into her parents' bedroom and showed us her father's pistol. She'd been babysitting Sam, and we'd been climbing the retama tree in my front yard. We were wearing our camouflage with pellet rifles slung over our shoulders, pretending to be mercenaries. She'd called across the street, "Y'all want to see something cool?" The pistol was a German Luger 1908, a semi-automatic. We'd read about them in our magazines.

"He burned himself," I told Matt. "He's sedated in intensive care, but he's going to pull through." I made up the last part. The night before, I'd asked my father about Sam and he told me to concentrate on my schoolwork and not to give Roscoe any more tuna.

"I heard he did it in the game room," Matt said. "I heard there's a gnarly bloodstain under the pool table."

"You heard from who?"

"Jeff Deyo," Matt said.

"You don't know Jeff Deyo," I said. Jeff Deyo was a red-eyed senior, a friend of Julio's who'd gotten held back. He wore the same flannel shirt every day, unbuttoned and tattered, and when I passed him in the hall, I smelled the smokers' patio.

"We've been hanging out," Matt said. "We've been getting high. If you tell, I'll kick your ass."

"You need to come get all my gear. If you don't want it, I'll throw it away."

"Don't take it out on me just because your girlfriend's brother blew his face off."

"She's not my girlfriend," I said.

"Right," he said, laughing. "She's dating Mr. Mitchell and you're with Anastasia from across town."

"You're an asshole."

"Check the game room," he said. "I heard the stain looks like a pot leaf."

Later that night, Mrs. Hensley called. My father was working his shift at Sears, and I was watching television on the couch while my mother smoked beside me. After answering, my mother handed me the receiver and told me to hang up once she switched to the kitchen phone. While she made her way down the hall, I told Mrs. Hensley about Roscoe catching the pine cones I tossed. She thanked me and said Holly would call me once things calmed down with Sam. Then my mother said, "Okay, Joshie, I got it."

"Okay," I said, but I just pushed the mute button and stayed on the line. I wanted to hear if Mrs. Hensley would say anything more about Holly, if she'd mention Mr. Hensley's Luger.

"We're going to Houston," Mrs. Hensley said. "They're moving him to the burn unit there."

"Okay," my mother said. "Okay."

"I don't know. I don't know if it's okay."

"Are the doctors saying anything else?"

"You're going to Houston, that's what they're saying. They're saying, We can't help him here."

I checked out the game room carpet on Saturday morning, then crept through the rest of the house that night. I knew I wouldn't find a bloodstain, just as I knew stealing through their hallways was a betrayal, but I couldn't stop myself. The moonlight canting through the blinds was bright enough in most rooms, but I also used the angle-head flashlight I'd bought at a gun expo. In the near-dark, the Hensleys' house seemed smaller, not bigger, which surprised me. A fine layer of dust on the surfaces—the marble-topped dressers, the pool table's rails, the framed pictures on the walls—shone in the light, reflected it, and made me think of silt on a riverbed. Moving through their rooms gave me a jumpy, underwater feeling, as if I were swimming through the wreckage of a sunken ship, paddling from one ruined space to another. I avoided Sam's room.

And I'd told myself I wouldn't go into Holly's room, but on Sunday night I did. The moon hung low in the sky, a lurid glow seeping through her curtains and puddling on the carpet. The room smelled of lavender. I'd been in there before, but stripped of noise and electric light, the layout seemed unexpected. Her bed was made, piled high with frilly pillows and stuffed animals—open-armed bears, mostly, and a plush snake stretching the length of her mattress. Four silver-framed photos topped her vanity: Holly and Sam in an orange grove, Julio on Padre Island flexing his arms and smirking, Roscoe licking Holly's face with her eyes closed, and a picture of Holly when she was younger, eating ice cream with a fork. Green and white streamers were tacked to her closet door, and when I moved too quickly, they fluttered and startled me. She had a banana-shaped phone on her nightstand, and I began worrying it would ring. Or I thought my father would silently appear in her doorway, his eyes narrow with disgust. *Leave,* I thought. *Go home.* In my chest, my heart was wild as a trapped, frantic bird.

And yet I stayed. Outside, Roscoe trotted around the pool; his tags tinkled. Once, he started barking and I dropped to the floor and crawled under Holly's bed. The Hensleys, I knew, had returned from Houston. I imagined Holly coming into her room and calling someone—Julio or maybe even Mr. Mitchell—to relay news about Sam. I imagined her turning off the lights and weeping and falling asleep with me under her. I considered bolting, trying to climb out the window and into the backyard, but knew I'd make too much racket. Roscoe kept barking. He was racing from one fence to another. I held my breath. I listened to phantom footfalls, the murmur of floorboards and studs behind the walls, the sad and random noises of an empty house at night. My hands were trembling, so I tucked them between my chest and the carpet. I still had the same underwater feeling, though now it was as if I were sinking, watching the surface grow blurry and distant. I waited to hit the bottom, to be discovered in the darkness.

But the lights in Holly's room never came on, and eventually Roscoe settled down. I pulled myself out from under the bed. I thought of how Matt and I used to crawl on our bellies in the brush behind his house, our faces obscured with mud. It occurred to me that while I was hiding in the Hensleys' house, he might be getting high with Jeff Deyo, and I felt suddenly and intensely alone. I had an odd sense of erasure, as if I were seeing the set for a play be dismantled. It was disorienting. And now that I'd crossed into Holly's room, I knew I'd return every night. The knowledge left me feeling resigned and melancholy, but also shot through with boldness. Before leaving, I dialed Matt's number on the banana phone, and when he answered, I didn't say a word.

My father was off from Sears that Thursday, so when he got home from the base, we mowed the Hensleys' lawn. Maybe my mother had asked him to do it, or maybe he'd gotten the idea after finishing our yard. I hoped it meant the Hensleys would return soon. As he pushed our lawn mower across the street—the engine idling, the blades scattering debris like when a Chinook lifts off—I followed him with the rake and bag of clippings.

A cold front had silvered the sky, unraveled the clouds. Every so often a wind would gust and eddy the fallen leaves. I waited for my father to announce the Hensleys were driving home from Houston, but he never did. While he swept the back patio, I said, "Maybe when Sam comes home Mom will quit smoking."

He leaned the broom against the house and fished his handkerchief out of his pocket, wiped his forehead. Roscoe was snortling along the fence line. I looked at my shoes, flecked with cut grass.

I said, "Maybe she'll be less stressed and—"

"Josh," he interrupted, "when Sam comes home, he might not look the same. We need to start preparing ourselves for that."

I nodded and dragged the rake across the yard; the trimmings jumped like grasshoppers. I thought of the picture in the silver frame on Holly's dresser, the one of her and her brother in the orange grove. Originally, I'd assumed they were in Florida, but now I believed they might have been in the Rio Grande Valley. In the picture, they're holding hands and heading away from the camera so their faces are invisible. It had become my favorite thing in Holly's room. Since Sunday night, I'd laid on Holly's bed, opened her closet to press my nose into her clothes, even spritzed her perfume on my windbreaker so I could inhale her at home. I'd dialed every number I could think of on her banana phone—my mother at the dry cleaner's, my father at the base and Sears, the secretary at King and the principal and my own house—then hung up when anyone answered. I never looked in her drawers, and I never stole anything, but every night I considered taking the orange grove picture.

"He's behind the eight ball," I said.

"This kind of thing can tear up a family," my father said. "It can rip even a strong family to shreds. It's not easy to watch."

"They need our help," I said. "You're saying we need to—"

"We'll help however we can, Josh, but what I'm saying is we're not going to let them drag us into their problems."

"I understand," I said, though I didn't.

"What I'm saying is when Holly needs a shoulder to cry on, don't let it be yours."

. . .

But the Hensleys didn't come home. Mrs. Hensley, I knew, called my mother late at night every couple of days, and I kept hoping to wake up and see their van in their driveway, but it never appeared. One night, I overheard my parents talking about skin grafts and a neoprene bodysuit that would keep Sam's flesh hydrated, compressed. Their voices were hushed and somber. My father also mentioned how Mr. Hensley's sick leave and vacation days were long gone. Another night, I thought they were talking about Sam again, but they were just discussing the breakdown of talks between President Reagan and Gorbachev in Iceland. The neighborhood started getting ready for Halloween, carved pumpkins appearing on porches and cardboard witches hanging in windows, and the temperature was dropping, especially in the evenings. In Corpus, the fall is damp and clammy. I laid out a pallet of blankets for Roscoe in the garage and started pouring warm water over his food. I used the copper-bottomed pot that Holly's father had left in the sink.

I'd barely seen Matt since the day we talked about the bloodstain. He'd been skipping school a lot, and on those days when I did glimpse him in the hall, I hid behind my locker door or ducked into the bathroom. With the changing weather, he'd taken to wearing a plaid flannel shirt with his fatigues. He hung out on the smokers' patio in the mornings and afternoons. I called his house every night from Holly's banana phone and never said anything. Sometimes Matt hung up right away, others he'd lay the receiver beside a radio he'd tuned to a Tejano station or he'd read classified ads from *Soldier of*

Fortune into the phone: *The survival knife you've been waiting for, ten-inch blade and hollow compass-topped handle. Bounty hunting is legal and profitable! Silent firepower: crossbows and slingshots.* The duffel bag with my warfare stuff was still in my room, and though I no longer expected Matt to take it away, I also hadn't unpacked it.

So, on the morning when he waved me over to the smokers' patio and said he'd pick up the duffel that afternoon, I should have been relieved. There were a few other students on the patio, sallow-skinned seniors I'd seen with Holly and who'd always intimidated me. I was surprised by how easily Matt fit in. He was wearing his tigerstripe camos, toeing out a cigarette with his combat boot. He blew smoke over his shoulder, the way my mother sometimes did, and said, "Is that cool? Jeff said he'd give me a ride."

"I threw it away," I said.

"No way," he said, his voice awash with disappointment, as if I'd forgotten his birthday.

"I didn't think you were coming. I was tired of seeing it."

"That really sucks, Josh."

"And there wasn't a bloodstain," I said.

"What?"

"At Holly's house," I said. "Sam didn't shoot himself."

"That's what this is about?"

"I looked. There's no bloodstain," I said. "He burned himself with a pot of water. He'll probably have a skin graft."

Matt nodded, his eyes downcast and thoughtful. A small wind picked up, wafting the acrid smell of put-out cigarettes. I thought Matt was thinking of something kind to say about

Sam. Once, when I got stung by an asp behind his house, he broke off a piece of aloe from his mother's plant and rubbed it on the wound.

Now, though, he just grinned and said, "I bet his face looks like melted cheese, all stretched and gooey. He won't need a mask for Hallowe—"

My fist connected right above Matt's temple. "Oh shit," a girl said, and a crowd of smokers cinched around us. Before Matt knew what was happening—before *I* knew what was happening—I'd hit him again in his mouth. Already there was blood on his teeth, in the corners of his lips. Then I was on top of him and we were falling to the patio and he was trying to cover his face with his forearms and saying "Dude, come on, stop, no," and I was waiting for someone to stop me, to pull me off of him, to save both of us.

The principal called my mother at the dry cleaner's to pick me up from school; he'd suspended me for three days. I expected her to be angry or embarrassed, but when I apologized to her, she said, "Oh, Joshie, we always thought Matt was a twerp."

We drove to the bayfront and sat on the seawall. Although we were out in the open—the bay seething in front of us, the docked sailboats bobbing in the marina to the west—I felt as if we were hiding, staking out a place to plot our next move. The tide heaved. Waves walloped the barnacled pylons; the dirty foam spread and dissolved. Eventually a crisp, salted wind nosed ashore and my mother scooted closer to me. I kept expecting her to light a cigarette.

"Sometimes I snoop in the Hensley house," I said.

"I know."

"You do?"

"I watch your little flashlight beam from our window," she said. "It reminds me of a fly trying to get out."

"I don't take anything," I said. "I just look."

"I know that, too."

A white gull hovered over us, then banked off and wheeled over the surf. I could hear cables clanging against hollow masts in the marina, the wind soughing through the dry palm trees that loomed along the seawall. Behind us stood the Memorial Coliseum where the gun expos took place. My knuckles ached.

"Dad says Sam might look different when he comes home," I said.

My mother nodded. She was watching the gull. It had landed on a pylon, its head moving around in twitches.

"And he said I should stay away from Holly."

"Her life's already sewn up," she said, her gaze still trained on the gull. "Matt's is, too. And now probably Sam's."

"I don't understand," I said.

"Good," my mother said, resting her head on my shoulder. "Good, I'm glad."

Now, I think of 1986 as the year my life pivoted away from what it had been, maybe the year when all our lives pivoted. It was the year my parents spoke in low, furtive tones and I strained to hear what they weren't saying. It was the year I surrendered the weapons of my youth—the morning after I fought Matt, I *did* throw out my duffel bag—and the year Holly Hensley shocked everyone by dropping out of school and joining the coast guard. This happened right after Thanksgiving. Her enlisting, I remember, was met with disillusionment and disdain—it seemed selfish and rash—but she found her footing in the military and enjoyed a distinguished career. After the coast guard, she moved to the army and was stationed in Hawaii, Guam, and, until her chopper went down two days ago, Afghanistan. According to the short obituary my mother just emailed me, Holly is survived by two sons and a husband, and she achieved the rank of staff sergeant. I hadn't seen her in almost twenty years. Funeral arrangements are being made in Corpus. I'll send flowers, and if I can find it, I'll make a copy of the orange grove photo and mail it to her family.

The night after I got suspended, I decided to steal that picture of Holly and her brother. I'd been lying on my bed earlier that day—my father had taken away my stereo and television privileges, and until my suspension ended, I was only allowed out of the house to feed Roscoe—and I'd thought having the orange grove photo might quell my desire to sneak into Holly's room. I'd also started thinking Mr. Hensley would return soon, so my access to the house felt fleeting, like a journey to a foreign country—a deployment—was coming to an end. I wanted a souvenir.

The moon was full that night, lamping the Hensleys' backyard and rimming the curtains in Holly's room. Everything else lay in deep shadow; I clicked my flashlight on and off to see, and wondered if my mother was watching from across the street. I suspected she was and didn't mind. The house still smelled of potpourri, a little dank. I'd debated grabbing another picture from Holly's parents' room to replace the one I wanted to take, but finally decided I'd just cluster the remaining three photos and hope Holly would have forgotten what had been there before. It seemed possible.

I was standing in front of her dresser, trying to visualize the most inconspicuous way to rearrange the pictures when, from behind me, I heard, "What's buzzin', cousin?"

I spun around, knocked into the dresser. The frames toppled. My heart kicked in my chest. Holly was on her bed, lying on her side among the stuffed animals. Even when I looked straight at her, her image was obscured in the dark.

"I didn't take anything," I said.

"You should have," she said. "I would."

"I just like the picture of you and Sam in the orange grove."

"I do, too," she said. "What you can't see is that the oranges are frozen solid. It was last year, right before we came back, and there was this massive cold snap that killed everything."

I clasped my hands behind my back; they were trembling again. I said, "I'm sorry for sneak—"

"We're alone here, if you're wondering," she said, shifting on the bed. "My parents are still in Houston with Sam. Julio came to get me. If I don't go back to school, I won't graduate."

"I'm suspended," I said.

"And Matt's a bloody mess."

"You heard?"

"I heard you were defending Sam," she said. "I almost went to your house to thank you, but then I saw the grass clippings on the carpet and figured you'd be back."

"I never looked in your drawers," I said.

"You'll do better next time," she said.

A raft of clouds floated past the moon, shrouding the room for a moment. I looked at the ceiling and couldn't see it. I could hear myself breathing.

"I wanted the orange grove picture," I said. "I was going to steal it."

"You can't have that one, but I'll make you a copy," she said. "Want anything else?"

"I want Sam to get better."

"Me, too. He's trying. Anything else?"

"I want to know about Mr. Mitchell," I said.

Holly rolled onto her back. She tossed a stuffed white bear into the air, caught it, then did it again. She said, "I'll tell you, but you only get three wishes. You're sure this is how you want to use your last one?"

I wasn't sure of anything at that moment. I felt as if I was balancing on a precipice, and I needed to think clearly. I tried to imagine how disappointed my father would be if he knew where I was, tried to understand what my mother had meant about everyone's lives being sewn up. I thought of how Sam used Holly's sweatshirt for a blanket, and the baseball cap she'd given him for his birthday. I wondered how it would feel to live outside of Texas, what it would be like to walk through a frozen orange grove or to dowse yourself with boiling water or to see your young son lying in a coma and not recognize him.

And then, like that, I understood. Before I could stop myself, I said, "He's yours, isn't he? Sam is."

Holly tossed the bear again, higher. In the air, it spiraled and looked like a silver fish flashing through murky water. She did it again, higher still. I thought she was trying to hit the ceiling I could barely see.

"That's why you went to Florida," I said. "Your parents didn't want—"

"Josh," she said.

"Yes?"

"Stop talking," she said.

"I won't tell anyone."

"Come here," Holly said. "Just come here."

I thought I would lie beside her and she would whisper the trajectory of Sam's life to me, explain who else knew her secrets and who his father was. It gave me a sensation of inertia, of countless mysteries parting around me like currents. But Holly offered none of this. She just lifted the comforter and I took off my shoes and she pulled me on top of her. We kicked her stuffed animals to the carpet, stripped off our clothes, tangled into each other. Roscoe barked in the backyard and ran along the fence; Holly said, "He chases possums." The house groaned. I shivered. I thought of the Luger in her parents' bedroom and wondered where Matt was at that late hour. I worried my father would come looking for me, but also felt certain my mother would run interference. Soon, Holly said, "I just want him to be okay," and started sobbing against my chest. I was fourteen years old, scared and inexperienced and mystified by the luck of my life, and though I could think of nothing to say, I held her close, as tight as I could. Eventually her breathing slowed so completely I wondered if she'd gone to sleep. I hoped so. I was wide awake, my eyes open and adjusted to the darkness. The edges of her curtains were again framed in moonlight, and in the shallow glow, our skin looked new and smooth and unblemished, ready for the scars that were lying, somewhere, in ambush.

PALOMINO

—for Joe A. Martinez

The man and his wife came into Checkered Flag Auto just as I was locking up. He wore shorts and orthopedic shoes and a yellow T-shirt with the sleeves cut off. She was still in church clothes, heels and a floral dress, and she must've brushed her long hair and applied makeup just before getting out of their little Mazda coupe. I let them in because I hadn't made my quota for the month. I also didn't have anywhere better to be.

The man was beaded with sweat. He pulled a bandanna from his back pocket and blotted his face. His wife appraised the office—a wood-paneled trailer with two desks and a gurgling water cooler—like she was hoping to move in; I half expected her to start taking pictures with her phone. The man offered her the bandanna, but she declined with a demure wave. He shrugged as if to say, *Your loss.*

Then he said, "We want a look-see at your palomino out front."

"We know it's after hours," his wife said, "but Mr. Haslam loves old trucks."

"No arguments here," I said.

"See?" the man said to his wife as I plucked the keys from the pegboard. "*Motivated*."

I didn't know what he meant by that, but I liked him calling our '86 Chevy a palomino. It reminded me of old-timers who nicknamed boys "chief" and "sport." The truck was on consignment: two-tone tan and brown, mileage north of two hundred thousand, a long-bed Silverado that had sat on the lot for months. I lowered the price every few weeks, posted and reposted Craigslist ads. Just yesterday, the boss said, "You'd better sell that sorry son of a bitch before I set fire to it and collect insurance."

But now I was getting the headlong rush that comes when a customer's on the hook. It could've been that the man was retired and wanted a project. Or he was buying a kid's first car. Or he needed a beater for a ranch. Show me a man who can't find an excuse to waste money on an old pickup, and I'll show you someone not long for Texas.

As we crossed the lot, I bragged on the Chevy: one owner, AC still blowing cold, two gas tanks and no rust. I didn't say that the ball joints and driveshaft yoke were rotted out or that the timing was shot or that it leaked so much differential fluid that their driveway would shortly look like an abstract painting. I said the tags were current and the tires had good tread. I said I had paperwork for all the repairs that had been done over the years.

When I unlocked the doors—pointing out the power locks and windows—the man and his wife just stood there, holding hands and gawking, like they were on a game show and I'd just revealed their prize haul. I wondered if they were millionaires.

Over our heads, the ZERO DOWN pennants snapped in the wind. The traffic on the highway sounded like waves plowing the shore. Checkered Flag was half an hour from Corpus. Our slogan was "Drive a Little, Save a Lot."

"She's a smooth ride," I said. "The owner used to put her morning coffee on the floorboard and not spill a drop on the way to work."

"She's a palomino," the man said. He set to circling the truck, regarding it. He whistled.

His wife hung back, affording him privacy. She tossed her hair over her shoulder and the vanilla scent of her perfume wafted. She said, "You're a gentleman to stay late. I told Mr. Haslam that whoever was here would be needing to run home for Sunday dinner, but he said used-car salesmen are motivated."

"The customer comes first at Checkered Flag," I said.

"Hospitality you can hang your hat on, that's what Mr. Haslam says," she said.

Her voice was wistful, and for reasons I couldn't name, I understood the man wasn't her first husband. She'd been jilted, had suffered men who didn't appreciate her. She'd been beautiful once, that much was obvious, but she'd survived it. Now she was content, living a decent little life. The diamond on her ring was smaller than I expected.

"Every Sunday," she said, "we pass by and Mr. Haslam asks why anyone would put such a fine palomino out to pasture. Sometimes he'll ask at dinner or when we're watching our shows. For him, it's a gripping whodunit."

"People just decide they want newer things," I said. "They move on but leave good stuff for the rest of us."

"Let's giddyup," the man said. He'd staked himself by the driver's side door. "Let's see how the old saddle sits."

I tossed him the keys, a move I immediately regretted, but he caught them clean and I knew he liked his wife seeing it. I thought: Money in the bank.

His wife hurried to the passenger's side—or tried to. Her high heels teetered like she was on cobblestone. I worried she'd snap an ankle. When the man hefted himself in, the truck felt it. The steering wheel notched into the soft swell of his gut. He labored to reach down and slide the seat back; it required considerable effort, and once he got situated, he needed a rest. He dabbed his face with the bandanna while his wife climbed in.

I expected the man to crank the ignition and blast the AC, but what he did was drape his thick arm across the top of the bench seat and face forward. Like he was settling into a Jacuzzi. Like he was on a couch in front of a fireplace. His wife scooted toward him and nestled under his shoulder. He kissed her head. Strands of her hair webbed to his sweat-sheened face.

Together, they looked up at the headliner and then down at the dashboard. She opened the glove box, shut it. The same with the ashtray. She fiddled with the radio knobs and air vents, maybe just to make sure she could reach them from her position. He adjusted the rearview mirror, pressed the accelerator, tapped the brakes. Then they tilted their heads together and exchanged words I couldn't hear; I felt like I'd happened upon strangers in a private moment and should turn away. They conspired long enough for another wave of traffic to pass, then he straightened up and put his left hand on the wheel. She leaned against his shoulder, rested her hand on his knee. They looked like they were on a lazy drive, watching the open country whoosh by, posing for a portrait of what happiness could be.

I'd waited a year before deciding to sell it. I kept remembering how we'd park outside the airfield, how we'd lay on our backs in that long bed and watch the pilots practice touch-and-go landings, how you'd get scared and koala onto me. And the time we drove it to Choke Canyon and saw that stray dog rooting around the truck-stop garbage cans, how you came out of the store with two roast beef sandwiches, not for us but for him. And how every night after work, for that whole long year, I'd see the truck in the driveway and for a moment I could forget that you'd left.

"Where do we sign, sheriff?" the man said. I hadn't noticed him and his wife getting out of the truck, but they were in front of me again. He said, "Where do I scratch my X?"

"Do what?" I said. I was sweating, jelly-kneed, lightheaded.

"We're ready to take this filly home," he said.

"You didn't even turn the key," I said. "You haven't even raised the hood or kicked the tires."

"We've taken up enough of your time," he said. "We're ready to ride into the sunset."

"You're very generous to stay late with us," she said. "Mr. Haslam has had his eye on this palomino for a long while."

The pennants were being bullied by the wind, flipping over themselves, tangling up. I imagined the boss noticing the truck gone in the morning, imagined which car he'd park in its place.

"Why do you keep calling it a palomino?" I asked.

"The only thing Mr. Haslam loves more than an old truck is a good horse."

"Let's go to the rodeo," the man said. "Let's do-si-do."

"It leaks differential fluid," I said. "The gearbox might as well be mesh."

"Never look a gift horse in the mouth, I'll tell you that," he said.

"The timing's off. It'll strand you where you stop."

"Mr. Haslam can't believe she's been here as long as she has. We feel blessed."

I wanted to ask them how long they'd been married, how they solved for all the variables, what they'd figured out that we hadn't. Instead I said, "It needs new brakes, a whole new front end."

"She's got colic and wants some TLC," the man said. "I'm chomping at the bit."

"Mr. Haslam is good with tools. He's excellent with—"

"The ball joints are rotten. The driveshaft is ready to fall out. The old owner spilled her coffee on the floorboard every morning. There are stains under the mat."

"A cowboy never lets his horse drink water he wouldn't drink himself," he said.

"I don't know what you're saying," I said. "I don't know why you keep talking about cowboys and horses."

The man screwed up his face, like I'd started speaking a dead language. He said, "Have you got another desperado raising the ante? Is that it? How about an extra five hundred?"

"I can't do it," I said.

"We've got cash money right here," he said, and like that, his wife slipped her purse from her shoulder and went for her wallet. She was peeling off bills in no time. Her perfume wafted again. Her hair dangled like a broken wing.

"I've already shut down the system," I said, hoping to sound definitive and professional. The closest thing we had to a system was the window unit that sputtered water when we ran it too long.

"This is like no horse-trading I've ever done," he said.

"I'm sorry," I said, and I was.

"You're a highwayman," he said. "You're a low-down—"

"Keep the keys," I said. The idea must have been forming for a while—maybe an hour, maybe a year—but I could only see its full shape now. Just then I felt sure of myself, the future. And I felt like I'd already wasted too much time. I said, "Come back in the morning."

"How about another seven fifty?" he said. "Straight into your saddlebags, just between two cowboys and a little lady."

"I'll be here by eight. I usually bring doughnuts," I said, not a word of it true. I still had a key for the truck on my key chain—the one with the guitar bottle opener from our Nashville trip—and I was already wondering how long it would take the boss to realize I wasn't coming back, how long it would take me to drive to wherever you were.

"An extra grand," he said. "Final offer. No one else will pay anything close to that for an old swaybacked mare."

"We'll square up tomorrow, pardner," I said. "Your palomino will be raring to go at sunup."

The man squinted at me, then at his wife, then back to me. It could've been that he hoped she and I were pulling one over on him, that we'd been haggling all this time and she'd already paid and we three were about to start celebrating. He bit the inside of his cheek and shook his head. The heat bore down. The wind barreled over us. The man started to say something, then quit. He turned and walked toward their little Mazda. He paused to wring out his bandanna. I hoped he'd tie it on his face outlaw style, or come back and spit on my boots, call me a yellowbelly. He didn't.

His wife stayed put. She was glaring at me, furious and aghast and unwavering. Her hair whipped across her eyes and she didn't blink. I figured she was about to cry or curse or slap me. She had the right. But I also suspected she'd hear me out if I told her our whole story. She'd soften. She struck me as a woman who'd been accused of impulsiveness in the past, of loving too blindly. I thought: You're one of my kind.

Overhead, the snapping pennants sounded like rifles being cocked. The highway was quiet, but in the distance was the gathering rumble of traffic, a stampede that would soon overtake us. I wanted to apologize again, to plead my case, to receive her blessing and light out on the road. All she wanted was to buy your truck, the one you and everyone else had told me to sell. She didn't speak or flinch. Neither did I. We were in a corral, the late sun casting shadows of stallions and quarter horses and the old palomino at our feet. We were a few paces apart. We were gunslingers waiting to draw. We were about to lay everything we had on that lonely line.

DIXON

A star-smeared night, the usual briny and humid haze of the brush country in August, and Dixon was hauling twenty cases of stolen toys up from the Rio Grande Valley. They were in the bed of his truck under a blue tarp. He took care to drive the speed limit and flash his blinker. If the border patrol at the Sarita checkpoint asked, he'd claim a delivery mix-up. If the guards were white, they might not even stop him.

The toys had been slated for Dairy Queen kids' meals, a promotion for a book series called *Pegaterrestrials* in which the characters were half alien and half winged horse, but that morning the office phone rang and a collectibles dealer had offered three grand for the lot. Dixon was forty-four and he'd managed the franchise outside Harlingen for four years. He knew he'd be fired, maybe arrested, too, but he also knew better than to give himself time to reconsider. He loaded the cases into his truck between customers. When the afternoon crew arrived, he went to the filling station to top off the tank. He checked his tire pressure and brake lights. Then he drove to the house and had supper with his wife, hamburger meat fried with peppers and onions. Afterward, they ate Blizzards he'd brought home for dessert and he told her not to wait up.

Dixon pressed his swollen knuckles to the cold paper cup and felt a soothing. Trish saw it, looked away. She said, "You're doing all this for someone named Cornbread?"

"I'm doing it for the money. Three grand gets us closer to the twenty-eight days."

"Three grand from a man named after bread you cook in a skillet," she said.

"Sounded more teenager than man."

"Where does a teenager get that kind of cash?"

"Where does anyone?"

Trish licked her red plastic spoon. She said, "Did you put the pistol back in the truck?"

"I'm doing it for Katie," he said. Their daughter was fifteen. She'd been asleep in her bed since Dixon had carried her there the night before.

"A man got arrested this morning," Trish said. "He was driving a hearse and had dope in the cadaver, an old woman stuffed full of pot."

"He didn't think the creek would rise."

"I never understand what you mean by that."

"My father used to say it," Dixon said. He wanted to get going. The deal was to meet Cornbread at a Kingsville taxidermy shop by ten. He said, "It means we'll be all right."

"If your knuckles aren't broken, they're getting close. I can put some ice in the cooler for your drive."

"After I get home," he said.

"Part of me wishes you hadn't gone so easy on those boys."

"I doubt that's the word they'd use."

"You know my meaning, Dixie," she said.

"I need to scoot," he said.

"The man with the hearse probably figured the cadaver would confuse the dogs," Trish said. She was rinsing the plastic spoon. Their drawers were full of Dairy Queen flatware.

"What time do they start admitting patients at Bayview?"

"The story was on the news," she said. "It happened at Sarita. That's all I'm saying. It happened where you're fixin' to go."

His headlamps washed out on the pavement. The air pushing through the vents smelled of creosote and trapped heat. Dixon wished the truck's radio still worked. He hadn't missed it for years, but tonight he wanted distraction. The drive was too flat, too dim and quiet. Occasionally, a sharp and radiating pain singed his knuckles; he should've accepted that cooler with ice. He alternated hands on the wheel. Outside Raymondville, plastic grocery bags were snagged on barbed wire fences. They looked like jellyfish.

How long since he'd come up this way? They used to go to Corpus for Katie's school clothes because Valley stores weren't up to snuff. There had been trips to see the replica Columbus ships dry-docked by the museum and the air shows at the army depot. Mostly, they'd drive up to go bird hunting near the King Ranch. For Katie's twelfth birthday, they'd given her a .20 gauge. Dixon taught her to press her cheek to the shotgun as she's patterning the dove, to keep her eyes on a shot bird as it falls, to track them where they like to eat—wheat fields and sunflower crops and gravel roads. He didn't know what other fathers did with their daughters; the greatest luck of his life was having the only girl he'd know how to raise.

An hour into the drive, his cell lit up on the passenger seat. Felipe, his assistant manager, had an irate customer.

"She's got three kids here," Felipe said. "They want the new toys."

"That promotion doesn't start until tomorrow. We aren't allowed to pop the cases earlier," Dixon said.

"I know, but the kids are losing their shit and we're trying to close. I thought I'd just slip her a couple, but I can't find them."

"Give her free Blizzards," Dixon said.

"We already shut down the machine. Before her, we hadn't had a customer for an hour. Did we move the cases?"

"Give them extras of the old ones."

"What about tomorrow? I'm scheduled to open and if the toys aren't here, I can't—"

"They didn't grow goddamn legs," Dixon interrupted. "Hell, Felipe, they didn't just walk out the goddamn door."

Before Eddie Milford, Katie's interest in boys had not extended beyond hunting experience—how old they'd been when they got their first guns, what kind of shells they loaded, how many birds they'd brought down in a day. She was in competition with them, not love. At fourteen, she still played cards and went bowling with her parents, made honor roll, washed dishes without being asked. So when the cop called Dixon last year, he figured it for a prank. Katie detained for panhandling? The word itself seemed vaudevillian: panhandling. And yet it was no joke. Others were on the hook as well, a crew of friends whose names neither Dixon nor Trish recognized. But the cops knew Milford. He was nineteen, a burnout. No question that he concocted the scam where the kids spread out through the mall, claimed to have been separated from their church group, and begged for bus fare money. Security footage showed they'd been running the con for weeks. Katie spent the day at the police station but got off with a warning. She cried and shook and apologized when Dixon picked her up, but he knew he'd been given a gift: She'd be too scared to court more trouble in the future.

But then came truancy notices and calls from Ivan at the pawnshop: Katie was hocking her mother's tennis bracelet, Dixon's circular saw, the .20 gauge she'd gotten for her birthday. Then came so many nights of her sneaking out her window that Dixon drilled it shut; he countersunk six screws from outside so she couldn't work on them from her bed. Dixon talked to her by himself, so did Trish, and they talked to her together. She saw a counselor at school and started reading books to old folks at the retirement home. Then she got suspended for fighting Sonia Santos in the cafeteria. Katie said Sonia had been the instigator, but only Dixon believed her. Trish accused him of cutting Katie too much slack, of seeing good where there was only shit. A month ago, Katie came home in a police cruiser with pupils the size of quarters. The cops had been called on a noise complaint and when they arrived at the apartment Milford shared with his brother, they found a bowl party.

"A what?" Dixon had asked the officer. Katie was still in the cruiser, her cheek pressed to the window.

"Kids dump a bunch of their parents' pills in a bowl, then spend the night munching on them like popcorn. No one ever knows what they're taking."

"Where's Milford?"

"County," the cop said. "His brother, too."

"How long?"

"Up to the judge. With all those pills, they might be in for a stretch."

"Too bad," Dixon said.

Then he crossed the yard and gathered his daughter from the squad car. She was dead weight in his arms, like her bones had turned to gruel.

Next time his phone buzzed, the night was full dark and the call lit the cab. Trish said, "Why are you the one on the road?"

"Do what?"

"If Mr. Cornbread wants his toys so bad, why didn't he make the drive down?"

"DQ has security cameras," he said.

"They're working again?"

"Safety first," Dixon said.

"This doesn't add up," Trish said. "We didn't think it out."

In truth, Dixon had suggested delivering the toys tonight because Cornbread said he wouldn't have access to a truck until next week. Waiting that long seemed careless, cowardly.

"I guess she hasn't emerged yet," he said.

"I checked on her. She kicked the covers off."

"She'll sweat some of it out. That's all to the good."

"She still smells like that glue," she said.

"It's in her hair," Dixon said.

"Like those resistoleros," she said. There'd been articles in the paper about homeless kids addicted to huffing Resistol across the border. The cobbler's glue was cheap and legal in

Mexico. It suppressed hunger. Dealers sold it in baby-food jars.

"She'll hate us more if they have to cut her hair to get it out," Trish said.

"Bayview will have better shampoo," he said. "She doesn't hate us."

"They start admitting at eight. I didn't answer you earlier."

"We'll be the first in line," he said.

"I made some tuna in case she wakes up wanting real food. I thought you might want some when you got home, too."

"Nothing would taste better," he said.

"Felipe called," Trish said. "I let the machine get it."

"We talked. He needed help closing out the register."

"How far to Sarita?" she said.

"Coming up," he said. "I can see the lights."

"I told you about the woman stuffed with pot, right?"

"Yes, ma'am," he said.

"Cornflake should've come here. You shouldn't be driving all that way. Your poor hands."

"I didn't want him to know where we live," he said.

"Maybe he was thinking along the same lines."

"We're all right," he said.

"That's what you keep saying," she said.

The Sarita checkpoint was bleached in artificial light. Dixon had to lower his visor as he idled behind a tractor-trailer being searched by two guards. One was white, the other was Mexican. Flashlights, clipboards, handcuffs, and sidearms. The Mexican guard led a German shepherd around the truck on a leash. He opened the trailer and waved his light inside: wooden crates of grapefruit. Dixon rolled down his window and the night swamped in, heavy as wet wool. He fidgeted with the vents. He could feel his pulse racing under his jaw. His knuckles were throbbing, too, and he concentrated on the pain as a way of calming himself. After a sedan pulled behind him, he realized he'd been considering reversing out and hooking a U-turn back to Harlingen.

The rig heaved into gear and rumbled out of the checkpoint. Dixon pulled up. The white guard stepped in front of the truck, waving him forward then motioning for him to kill the engine. Dixon considered asking if he could keep it running, explaining that the starter was on its last legs, but he turned the key instead. The guard flipped a switch in his booth and a strip of spikes hinged up from asphalt. The other guard set to circling the truck with the dog.

"Where you off to?" the guard asked.

"Kingsville," he said.

"Carrying any firearms or illegal drugs?"

"I've got a .38 under my seat," Dixon said, hoping such honesty would pay off later. He added, "Permit's at home."

The guard scratched a note on his clipboard just as the tailgate dropped down and rocked the whole truck. It was like jumping a curb. The guard with the dog whistled and his partner went to see what he'd found.

When the guard returned, he said, "What's with the boxes?"

"Toys for kid meals. I manage the Harlingen DQ. We got the Corpus shipment."

"You said Kingsville."

"I'm meeting another manager there. He's hauling them the rest of the way."

The guard surveyed the truck's cab: paper trash on the floorboards, sun-split dashboard, cell phone on the passenger seat. He glanced to the rear. In the mirror, the other guard shrugged. Dixon put both hands on the wheel, a mistake.

"What happened to your knuckles?" the guard asked.

"Punched the wall when I saw we got the wrong shipment."

"With both hands?"

"Not my finest hour," Dixon said. His shirt was soggy against the seat. If he floored the gas, he'd make it no farther than fifty feet past the spikes. Then, a memory: Katie used to love the sound of balloons popping. When she had chicken pox, Dixon had blown up a bag's worth of balloons and burst them with his pocketknife to make her laugh.

The guard had been talking. "Sir," he repeated, "I need to see your license."

Dixon took out his billfold. The guard checked the ID picture against his face. He wrote something else down, then passed it back.

"Can I get hold of the Corpus manager?" the guard asked.

"He's on the road. I don't know his cell, but his name's Milford. If he ever passes through, your time wouldn't be wasted searching his car."

"If he's got something to hide, we'll find it," he said.

"I heard about the hearse," Dixon said. "It's bad in the Valley, too—heroin, glue, pill parties."

"Is your firearm loaded?"

"Unloaded, it's just a paperweight."

"And if I make a call, I won't have trouble finding it registered in your name?"

"None at all," Dixon lied.

The guard held his gaze. He wasn't gauging whether Dixon was lying—Dixon suspected he knew the truth—but whether the infractions were worth his effort, whether whatever danger Dixon posed was tolerable. Without warning, the tailgate slammed shut. The guard moved to the booth and flipped the switch. The spikes flattened. The guards paced to the sedan behind him. Dixon had to crank the ignition three times before it turned over.

Excepting his pistol and Katie's .20 gauge, Dixon had sold all their guns. They'd gone one by one to the pawnshop—when he was short on rent, when the starter on the truck first gave out, when Trish's hours got cut at the deli counter. He kept the pistol because he'd never lived without one; the .38 had belonged to his father, had traveled from one house to the next with Dixon. He kept Katie's shotgun because it had once meant so much to her and he hoped it would again. After she tried pawning it on her own, he'd locked it in the gun cabinet in his and Trish's bedroom. The key was taped under his nightstand drawer.

For the last hour of the drive, he'd been thinking of Katie as someone suffering temporary amnesia. She was in a fugue state. Getting her out of this sludge could be as simple as reminding her of the life before. All he needed to do was jar her memory. He could manage it. They'd play cards and go bowling, they could even start hunting again, maybe head up to the

Hill Country where there was good pheasant shooting. If the taxidermy shop where he was meeting Cornbread did solid work, he'd have one of her birds mounted. Hang it above the television or in her room. When he'd laid her in her bed last night, Dixon was struck by how unfamiliar the room had become. Her plush toys and bright posters had been replaced by a wheel-less skateboard, a lava lamp, and barren walls. Maybe they'd hang a bird on all her walls, he thought now. Give her more to brag about, build her confidence. Trish would call his thinking naïve, but Dixon knew it would work. He could hardly wait.

The taxidermist's gravel lot was empty. A lamppost swayed over the squat building but the casing and bulb were busted. What little light there was spread from the Party Barn across the road. A line of cars ten deep waited at the drive-thru liquor store; one was an ice cream van. Before he stepped from the truck, Dixon slipped the pistol into the back of his waistband.

He thought about walking to the Party Barn to get a bag of ice for his knuckles but didn't want to risk missing Cornbread. He checked his phone and peered through the shop window. Cupping his hands around his eyes, he could make out mounted heads of deer, javelina, a caribou. He squinted but couldn't discern the quality of the work. A rattlesnake arrested in mid-strike, fangs bared. An armadillo on its back guzzling a Lone Star bottle. A lynx in a fierce pose, a marlin arching on the far wall, an owl spreading its wings. All the animals' dull glass eyes seemed fixed on Dixon.

When he turned from the window, a young man stood in

the street. He was pacing in the turning lane, trying to time his crossing. Cars barreled by in both directions and Dixon feared he'd be hit. After a minute without an opening, Cornbread tried darting out and forced a 4x4 pickup to swerve. The driver laid into his horn and kept on it for a hundred yards. Cornbread waved an exaggerated wave; it looked like he was trying to flag down a helicopter. Dixon wondered if he was on something. When traffic finally eased, Cornbread bolted across. He ran in a flailing, childish way. One of his shoes flew off and he had to kneel to retie it on a parking block.

"You're early," Cornbread said, bent at the waist, breathing heavy. He looked about Katie's age, but smaller. He said, "We're in line at the Party Barn. I didn't want you to think I flaked. I almost got run over by a truck."

"You brought the money?"

Cornbread dug in his pocket and came up with a roll of cash. Before handing it over, he doffed an imaginary cap. Dixon fanned it out—twenties, fifties, a few hundreds. He counted the bills twice, then again, arranging them to face forward. Cornbread had closed his eyes. His head bobbed to music only he heard.

Dixon said, "Help me get these boxes out of the truck."

Cornbread clapped his hands and cut a jig in the gravel.

They unhooked the tarp, lowered the tailgate, and began unloading. Cornbread worked as though he was still hearing the music, as though he could barely restrain himself from dancing. He looked not like a kid buying stolen toys, but like he'd randomly happened upon something he'd coveted for years. Once enough of the cases were on the ground, Cornbread swung himself into the truck bed and passed what remained to Dixon.

His phone vibrated. Trish's name appeared on the screen and he sent it to voicemail.

"We have a flea market booth," Cornbread said after they'd gotten all the boxes out of the truck. "We sell collectible toys. Each of these cases has one ultra-rare figure. Collectors pay out the ass for Pegaterrestrials."

"How old are you?" Dixon asked.

"Eighteen. I'm little for my age," he said.

"I thought you had to be twenty-one to buy anything at Party Barn."

"My friend's older," he said. "He's the ice cream man."

Dixon was trying to fold the tarp, awkwardly trapping a corner with his chin and getting nowhere, but when Cornbread noticed him struggling, he came to help. They folded it like a sheet, finished in no time.

Cornbread said, "We called about ten Dairy Queens before yours. I didn't think you'd show up."

An idea had been forming without Dixon's knowledge. It whorled outward as imperceptibly as a growing shell, recognizable only after taking its full and inevitable shape. Dixon said, "What about the extras?"

"Do what?"

"You said you sell the rare toys. What happens to the leftovers?"

"They're worthless. We'll blow them up with firecrackers."

"Sell them to me," Dixon said.

Cornbread looked toward Party Barn. The ice cream van was next in line.

"We'll pick out the ones you need, then I'll take the rest back to Harlingen," Dixon said. He felt awake and alive, sure of himself, the future. He said, "Five hundred for the lot?"

"Can we still have a few of the regulars to explode?"

"You bet," Dixon said. "Now show me how to spot the special ones."

Cornbread opened the first box, ferreting through the common figures until he found it. The toy was bright chrome—eagle wings, the muscled body of a Thoroughbred, an alien's smooth head and teardrop eyes. Cornbread studied it like a jeweler, handled it as delicately as he would a newborn chick. What drew children to such outlandish creatures? Dixon wondered. Had Katie read any *Pegaterrestrial* books? That he didn't know galled him. She'd always loved animals, declaring once that she wanted to be a zebra when she grew up, and in a way Dixon couldn't explain, he equated her hunting with an affection for the birds, an abiding desire to be closer with them. He'd ask her about such things when they drove to the Hill Country. Across the street, the ice cream van was entering Party Barn. Cornbread was still regarding the special figure with no small amount of awe. Dixon opened another box and located the chrome creature easily. Then he moved on to the next one, then the next and next. He opened case after case and his knuckles hardly hurt at all.

The day before yesterday Katie hadn't come home from school. They called her phone, left messages, waited. They paced the floor, stopping occasionally to part the blinds and watch the street, willing her to appear in the distance. Trish kept supper warm, then after a couple of hours they conceded to pick at their food in fraught silence. Every little noise sounded like the door opening. Finally, Dixon wiped his mouth with a DQ napkin and said, "I'll rustle her up."

He took the .38 from the gun cabinet and went to the Milford brothers' apartment. No surprise that they were gone, too. He lingered in the parking lot, but then set out. Trish was at home redialing Katie's phone. She called the hospitals and border patrol. She called the police who said nothing could be filed until Katie had been missing for twenty-four hours. She called Bayview Hospital, the rehab facility in Corpus, and scribbled rates on the back of an overdue electric bill: *28 days = 3600.00*. She called the morgue. The man who answered recognized their last name and said her husband had just left, said they'd get in touch if someone matching Katie's description arrived, said not to call back. She called Dixon to tell him whom she'd called and to ask where else he'd gone.

He'd gone to the mall and the pawnshop and her friends' houses. He stopped for gas and left the truck running for fear of it not starting again. He drove out to the citrus groves, her school, the retirement home where she read her books. He checked the underpasses where users camped. Nothing. Everywhere, nothing. His prevailing sense was of having always just missed her. No evidence supported it, but the notion of lagging one step behind weighed more heavily every hour. Phantom visions of her appeared in storefronts and on street corners. *Where are you, little girl?* he caught himself saying out loud. He'd emptied a tank of gas. The night was leaden, clouds scudded by and disappeared. Think, he thought. Think.

What he thought was this: The world is too goddamn big. If she'd headed out after the first school bell rang, she could've been in San Antonio by mid-afternoon, in Houston by supper, in Dallas by dusk. Or she could be within minutes of where Dixon was now. She could be unconscious or terrified or crying out for her father. He was near a motor court that rented by the hour when dizzying nausea took hold. He pulled to the curb and tried to vomit but nothing came. He stepped into the empty street and pivoted in a circle, as if scouting a spot to crouch in a field and wait for a flock of quail. The memory of her safety, of a life where he could trust the day to deliver her home, had withered and scattered. There were new rules now. Or the rules were unchanged and he'd failed to understand them until this moment.

He went to St. Pius where Katie had been christened. He prayed and lit a candle. He doubled back the way he'd come.

Dixon and Cornbread had culled the special figures from the cases by the time the ice cream van jostled into the parking lot. Headlights slashed across them, briefly whiting out the taxidermy shop's windows. The driver made a wide and fast arc that sent gravel pinging around, then reversed toward them. He braked and dowsed everything in a red glow.

The driver walked with a cane. He was shirtless, roped with skinny muscle, Dixon's age. His cigarette was near down to the filter. He extended his hand to Dixon and said, "Call me Moose."

"Moose and Cornbread," Dixon said.

"Sounds like an old-time meal," Cornbread said.

Moose smiled without conviction. Smoke rose into his eyes, but he seemed not to notice. He said, "Why are my cases open?"

"He wants to buy back the commons," Cornbread said. "We pulled the specials."

The tip of Moose's cigarette flared and smoke went through his nose. He caned his way over to the cases. He said, "What price are you offering?"

"I was thinking five hundred would do it. Cornbread says they're worthless."

"Worthless to us," Moose said, nudging a box with the tip of his cane, "but I'd wager they're worth a job to you."

"I could throw in another hundred."

"The price is a thousand."

"For something you're going to burn up with firecrackers?"

Moose squinted toward Cornbread, then Dixon. He said, "Then how about that pistol of yours? Would that square us?"

Dixon saw where this was going. He said, "We'll leave things be. Everyone can leave happy."

"I wish we could, bubba."

"Do what?"

"You decreased the value when you cracked the seals on the cases. They're not worth what I paid anymore. I'll need to collect a refund."

"My understanding was that you were only interested in the special figures."

"My understanding was that I was paying for unopened cases," Moose said.

"That's my bad, Moose," Cornbread said. "I just figured since the specials were what—"

"How about the three thousand," Moose cut him off, "your Saturday Night Special, your piece of shit truck, and we keep all the toys?"

"Our deal was for the cases and I delivered them," Dixon said and started for the truck. A line of traffic charged by and sounded like a long, heavy wave.

"Hey, bubba," Moose said, laughing. "I'm just jerking you. Of course you can have these no-nothing toys. How about six hundred and we call it a night?"

"Six hundred and we're done?" Dixon said.

"Six hundred and we'll hallelujah the county."

Dixon peeled off the cash. Moose grinned with the cigarette still clenched in his teeth—a show of shared enterprise—and limped over to take the money.

"How come you brought that pistol?" Moose said as Dixon loaded a case into the truck. "Didn't pick Cornbread for a friendly?"

"It's been a rough few days."

"Your knuckles tell that story just fine," Moose said.

Dixon expected Cornbread to help with the cases, but he stayed by the ice cream van. He was nothing but downcast eyes and stillness. No one spoke. For a while the only sound was gravel crunching beneath Dixon's boots.

Then Moose flicked his cigarette into the parking lot and said, "Thing is, bubba, I've had a rough few days, too, and the more I think about you toting a gun here, the more it chafes me."

"Selling those toys will cure that," Dixon said, stowing another case.

"It just makes me think you have untoward plans for me and my little buddy over there."

Dixon's back was to him. He closed his eyes and tried to figure the best move, tried to find some combination of words that would get him on the road.

"So, bubba," Moose said, "here's what's going to happen."

Dixon's eyes were still closed when he heard the air slicing behind him. The blow coursed through the hollows of his bones like quicksilver until there was too much weight to bear and Dixon felt the ground go out from under him. His chin cracked the tailgate as he fell. His mind pulled away from him, a reverse spiral as he hit the gravel. He thought of shot birds dropping from ice-blue skies. He thought of Katie in the back of the squad car with her eyes like coins, thought of her draped in a Texas flag, thought of limp and lifeless bodies filled with cold water and jellyfish, and then his thinking ceased and there was nothing except a soundless and enveloping blackness. Then, increasingly, not even that.

Last night, when he'd passed once more by the Milford apartment, the windows were leaking light. He drove onto the patchy grass and bounded up the concrete stairs two at a time. The door was slightly open. He pushed it the rest of the way with the barrel of the pistol.

A bucket of cobbler's glue sat on a wicker table, the air in the apartment thick with a viscous odor—the glue, yes, but also dank sweat and mildew, aerosol and rotting food, the ripe and chemical smell of semen. A Texas flag hung on the wall over a plaid couch pocked with cigarette burns. All the lights were on. A calico cat, likely a stray that had just come through the open door, was licking a grease-scabbed skillet on the stove. The cat paid him no mind. In the bathroom, the toilet seat was up and the water was dark with days of urine. Empty cans and bottles spilled from the tub. He took care where he stepped on his way to the bedroom. The door was shut, but he didn't want to hit a creaking floorboard; he tested each step before putting his full weight on it, as if worried the floor would collapse. What a time to think of how he and Trish used to tiptoe through the house after Katie got to sleep as an infant. Now, as then, he put his ear to the door. He heard a window unit working hard. He turned the knob slowly, bracing for when it clicked and he could peek inside.

Katie. Asleep on a bare mattress on the floor. No box spring. She wore an oversized T-shirt and nothing else. Even with only the slice of light from the hall, he could see that the soles of her feet were black with filth. The Milford brothers were naked beside her.

One of them lay curled in a ball and the other on his stomach. The room was freezing, sixty degrees at most. No pillows, no blankets. Another bucket of glue beside the bed. Used condoms on the carpet. He slipped into the room without lowering the pistol. His arm trembled. Sweat in his eyes, bile in his throat, the sense of standing on a threshold. Then came a harsh clattering racket from the kitchen, a sharp and ringing noise that quickly wobbled into silence—the cat had knocked the skillet to the floor. Dixon expected the noise to rouse one or all of them, but no one stirred.

Then Katie rubbed her face with the heels of her hands. She

yawned. She smiled, and it seemed an eternity since he'd witnessed such beauty. He hid the gun behind his back.

"Daddy," she said, groggy, "did you bring me a Blizzard?"

Before he could answer, her eyes lidded and she was back asleep. He lifted her from the bed and backed out of the room and carried her to the couch. The cat was cleaning itself on the wicker table. Dixon shooed it away. He snatched the flag from the wall and draped it over Katie. She snuggled into it, tucking the fabric under her chin. He kissed her cheek and whispered, "I'll be right back, Kaybird." He hadn't called her that in years, had entirely forgotten about the nickname, and yet, now, there it was. He took up the bucket of glue.

The brothers hadn't moved. The room was loud with the struggling air conditioner. He left the lights off, locked the door behind him, and beat the brothers until he lost feeling in his hands. Before he left, they were whimpering and pleading, huddled in different corners of the room, too disoriented to find their way out. Dixon flipped on the light. The brothers pressed their bloody faces to the walls. Whether out of fear or a reaction to the sudden brightness, Dixon didn't know. Nor did he know if they'd remember or understand what had happened once they sobered up. To make sure, he emptied a bucket of cobbler's glue over each of their heads.

He woke in the taxidermist's parking lot with gravel notching into his cheek. He coughed pieces of it out of his mouth like broken teeth and the coughing sent electric pain down his spine. He tried raising himself but couldn't. He was too heavy or weak or he'd forgotten how. His ears rang. He tasted copper and minerals and his own mealy blood. He tasted hamburger fried with onions and peppers.

He made it to his knees and stayed there. Saliva hung from his mouth to the gravel. The swelling on the back of his head felt like a bone spur, a cranial anomaly that had grown so fast it tore through the skin. There wasn't enough of him anymore. A breeze dragged itself over the parking lot, and when the air hit the gash, Dixon understood it was deep enough for his flesh to fold open. He thought he could feel grit in it. He reached to the top of his truck's tire and levered himself up. His eyes wouldn't focus. Then they did. The parking lot was abandoned. Party Barn had closed. His watch and phone were gone. His pistol, too, and the money.

But his keys were in his pocket, and when he turned to lean against the truck and rest a little, he saw that most of the toy cases were still there, too. He couldn't gauge if this was good or bad news. He tried to figure the odds of Moose returning, but his thoughts kept petering out. Too many angles to consider. They made his head throb. He loaded the cases as fast as he could, but all that bending over gave him vertigo. His vision kept twisting, shifting everything to the left. Each step was like trying to balance on a raft being pitched by waves. He draped the boxes with the tarp again, though not as thoroughly. He doubted it would hold to Harlingen.

He worried they'd taken his battery or cut the fuel line, worried the engine had given out again on its own, but the ignition cranked. After ten miles, he remembered to click on his headlights. The truck listed across the highway's double yellow lines, and when Dixon jerked back into his lane, the cases slid across the bed. He drowsed. He lowered his windows to fill the cab with wind and noise that would keep him awake. The truck rattled. Trish would say he should've known better. He felt like a man who'd stayed too long at the poker table, a man who should've quit while he was ahead.

Not that all was lost. He was making decent time. The drive was halfway done and the tarp was holding. There was no checkpoint heading south, and when Sarita passed on the other side and he saw his two guards doing their work, a particular relief washed over him: He didn't have to worry about them again. His head had eased up some. He felt one step removed from the current moment, which likely meant he had a concussion, but with that distance came clarity. The future seemed as certain as the past. He'd return the toys to Dairy Queen before going home and he'd keep his job. Trish would clean him up enough to get Katie admitted to Bayview, then they'd go to the minor emergency clinic. He'd scrounge the money for Katie's treatment before she was discharged from the hospital. He had almost a month. There were ways. Sell the truck. Visit Ivan at the pawnshop. Go to other Dairy Queens where he knew the managers, pluck the special figures from the cases, open up his own goddamned flea market booth.

When he pulled into the driveway, Trish was on the porch. She held her phone with both hands, which made her look like a woman praying. What Dixon believed was that their air conditioner had crapped out again, and he hated that his wife and daughter had been suffering through the soupy heat. He wondered if there was enough room on his credit card for a motel.

Even just a few hours of comfortable sleep would do them all a world of good.

"You look chewed up and stepped on," Trish said. "You look like you've been hit with a bag of nickels."

"Things could've gone smoother out there, I'll tell you that."

"I thought you were dead. You never called me back."

Dixon walked to the porch and she rose to inspect his wound. The blood on his shirt embarrassed him; he should've washed up at Dairy Queen after returning the toys. Trish had him bend into the floodlight. She said, "You need stitches."

"It'll keep till after Bayview," he said.

She cocked her head, confused, like he was a stranger who'd called her name on the street. He wondered if he'd slurred his speech, if the blow to his head was compromising him in ways he couldn't parse.

"I called the police," Trish was saying. "They came and took my statement."

Now Dixon was confused. Now she was the stranger calling his name. "Police?"

Trish said, "You didn't listen to my messages?"

"Cornbread brought reinforcements," he said. "They took my phone. The money and pistol, too, but we can still get her into—"

"Oh, Dixie," she interrupted. "Oh, honey."

"You were right. I didn't think it out. I should've had him drive up here and—"

"She's gone, baby. The cops are out hunting for her."

"Gone? What does *gone* mean right now?"

"Her window," she said.

"I had her window drilled shut."

"Someone undid it," she said. "They left the screws on her windowsill, standing up like little soldiers."

Dixon couldn't get his bearings. His eyes lit on his patchy yard, the dark neighborhood, the stars in the sky like buckshot and his wife talking under it. He felt connected to none of it, completely untethered.

"The last time I saw her was around eleven," Trish said. "She ate some tuna on the couch then went back to her room. I called to tell you."

"What time is it now?"

"Almost four."

"She could be in San Antonio. She could be halfway to Cancun," he said.

"We had a nice talk," Trish said. "She asked if you were mad and when you'd be back. Maybe she was distracting me while they undid her window, but she seemed sincere. I brushed some glue from her hair and she hugged my neck before going back to bed."

"I'm not mad at her," he said.

"I told her that," she said.

"Good," he said.

"I'm furious, though. I'm just seeing red, but I knew you'd be more forgiving."

She meant *too* forgiving. There was no disdain in her tone, but Dixon still heard the accusation: He'd been too timid, too relentless in his optimism, too faint of heart. Had he handled things differently, they'd be in a better spot now. He couldn't say she was fully wrong.

The morning was sticky, every surface beaded with condensation. First light was an hour away, but cars were already moving into the streets. People were heading to work or coming off overnights. Dixon wondered how he and Trish would appear to someone driving by. Like a couple whose air conditioner had died? Like they'd been up all night fighting? Or would the scene, in the shallow glow of the floodlight, look happier? Dixon could easily recall mornings like this when he was busy packing the truck to take Katie hunting. Trish had always woken up to see them off and they'd always let their daughter sleep until it was time to leave.

"Is there any tuna left?" Dixon asked.

"Plenty," Trish said. "She just had a few bites."

"I should eat something, then get cleaned up. She doesn't need to see me like this when she gets home."

"I'll run you a bath," she said. "It'll feel good to soak and I'll get a better look at your head that way."

"That sounds mighty fine," he said.

Trish went into the house. Dixon waited until light came through the bathroom window then he climbed the porch and made his way to their bedroom. The key for the gun cabinet was still taped under his nightstand drawer. Only now did he realize he'd been expecting otherwise. He listened for Trish coming down the hall as he took out the .20 gauge, but she was in the kitchen slicing a tomato for his sandwich. The smell of coconut bubble bath wafted; the tub was filling and Dixon hoped Trish would check the water before it flooded. He slipped out the front door quietly, concealing the gun with his leg. The morning was already brighter, a long seam of color on the horizon. His knuckles were aching again. His head thrummed and his vision undulated, as if he were watching the world through a fast-moving stream. But his thoughts were sharp, concerted. When he saw Trish pass from the kitchen and disappear down the hall, he dropped the truck into neutral and let it roll backward from the driveway. Of course, he worried the engine wouldn't crank, but it came to life without trouble. A promising sign, Dixon thought, a signal of good things to come.

YOUNG LIFE

You are thirteen, almost poor, afraid of the wrong things. A very partial list of what scares you includes being hit in the face with a baseball, dropping your lunch tray in the cafeteria again, never kissing a girl or seeing an albatross. You're actually sure you'll never kiss a girl, so what you're really afraid of is getting caught in a lie. There's also an illogical, subterranean fear that if a girl ever did agree to kiss you—maybe at, say, a charity kissing booth—you'd botch the whole shebang and word would spread through school like when you ate the Frito Pie you'd dropped because you didn't have enough money for another. The cover of Ozzy Osbourne's album *Speak of the Devil* scares you, as does the dentist and the whine of circular saws. You are not afraid of T.J. Godbout. T.J., who's been held back twice and steals wheelchairs from Kmart. T.J. who, last Halloween, dressed as a Klansman.

It's 1983. T.J. is sixteen and your parents say he won't see his next birthday. They say it every year. He's trash, they say, plain white trash. Like you're not. Like you don't usually eat Pop-Tarts for supper. They've forbidden you from hanging out with him, but they're never around so it doesn't matter. Your father leaves for weeks at a stretch, working oil rigs in the Gulf. Your mother cleans rooms at the Sand Dollar Motel and waits tables at The Kettle. Your grandmother also lives with you, but she's mostly blind and her head teems with ghosts. Sometimes she wanders off and you have to hunt for her in the neighborhood; a month ago, you found her twisting in the tire swing in Mr. Reyes's backyard. You read to her before bed, worrying you'll go blind, too.

You live in Ingleside, Texas, three sand-patched lawns down from T.J. He claims to have seen a concert in Corpus where Ozzy threw a puppy into the audience and refused to play until they ripped the dog apart. T.J. lies. He likes to be shocking. He says, I fucked Mrs. Borden in the teachers' lounge. He says, If I get held back again, I'll take my daddy's twelve-gauge and light up the school. T.J. walks everywhere because driver's ed is too expensive. He used to have a bike with mag wheels, one yellow and one red, but someone jacked it. Your parents say he was buying angel dust. You hope T.J. doesn't notice how you avert your eyes from *Speak of the Devil.* Instead, you peer through the glass of his aquarium. Loretta is a red-tailed boa, five feet long and still growing. She eats rats. When the pet store runs out of those, T.J. buys a hamster. You're afraid of Loretta, but she's why you visit as often as you do. You've held her on occasion and felt invincible.

The baseball-in-the-face fear always gathers before PE. The real terror here is losing some teeth. Missing teeth make you think of your grandmother's dentures, and her dentures make you think of growing old, and growing old makes you think of dying without ever kissing a girl.

But the baseball unit is halfway done and you've gotten this far without holding the bat. Fifteen more days and you're safe. Your baseball scam is simple: Every day after changing into your gym clothes—ammonia-reeking, a size too small—you book it into the outfield and stay put for every inning. Occasionally you field balls but no one, not even Coach Cantu, notices your absence in the batting order. When T.J. steps up to the plate, he says, "Back it up, boys, No Refund Godbout is fixin' to hit." No Refund is a nickname T.J. gave himself. Others are Big Gun, Big Chopper, and the Sorcerer.

Sometimes you catch yourself wishing Coach Cantu were your father. He drives a T-top Z28. When a student acts cocky—usually T.J.—Cantu arm wrestles him left-handed and wins. There's always a wallet-sized plug of Day's Work tobacco in his shorts pocket. He wears his hair slicked back and has a mustache like a broom. A glossy photo of Magnum P.I. hangs in his office, and to make students laugh, he styles his hair in front of it like a mirror. He says, Who's the handsome one now, Tommy? After you dropped your lunch tray, Cantu sat at your table. He gave you half his Coke.

"One of these days," he said, "all of these giggling donkeys will work for you."

The person you're most worried about seeing you eat a baseball is Margaret Shanahan. She sits in front of you in Texas History and you spend the hour trying to smell her ponytail. Because she might find it romantic, you want to tell her that certain albatrosses mate for life. You wonder how many guys she's kissed. On the baseball diamond, Margaret plays third base. In the outfield, you watch for when she sweats enough that the color of her bra shows through her Young Life shirt. Young Life is the youth ministry club popular girls join. You equate being born again with having money and straight posture, and though you can't recall the last Mass you attended, you hope Margaret never finds out your family's Catholic. Each of her school folders has *John 3:16* written on it. Her handwriting is disappointingly masculine. She prays before lunch.

On the last play before Coach Cantu tells everyone to hit the showers, T.J. cracks a home run that arcs so high you have to shield your eyes from the sun. The ball drops into the brush hemming the field. When T.J. rounds third base, despite being on the opposing team, Margaret high-fives him. She's wearing a bra so red that it gives you a head rush.

Last Halloween, your costume was the same as the year before: rubber werewolf mask and cut-up flannel shirt with red paint splattered on it for blood. When T.J. came to the door, you recognized his grubby sneakers under the white robe and thought he was supposed to be a ghost. It sunk you. You'd been counting on something elaborately horrifying, or at least disgusting, but the costume only proved he didn't have money for anything better. You pitied him, and the pity bullied you. T.J.'s father was a shrimper and gone more than yours. His mother had taken up with a man in Louisiana. You wanted to compliment T.J.'s pointy hood, his perfectly circular eyeholes. You were about to give him extra candy when your mother gasped. Then your father pushed through the door. He snatched off

T.J.'s hood and grabbed him by the ear and walked him down the porch. He said, "What's wrong in your head, boy? Just what the hell is the matter up here?"

Two days after Margaret wore her red bra, she's on T.J.'s porch, knocking on the torn screen door, tightening her ponytail. She frowns at the wheelchairs in the yard—their rims catch sunlight and turn it silver—then she steps inside. When she leaves, her hair is down. She has to work to pull her fingers through it.

Nights, you read encyclopedias to your grandmother. Your mother is assembling a set of Funk and Wagnalls, one a month, through a grocery store promotion. She got the set of ivy-stenciled dishes the same way. "My china," she calls it. So far the encyclopedias reach *G*.

Your grandmother doesn't care what you read, so you thumb pages until you find animal entries. You reread ones she's already heard without her noticing. She sits in her swivel rocking chair, foot tapping like she's listening to music, ashtray on her lap. Her dentures soak in a mason jar on the coffee table, and you work not to see them. Bees, you tell her, can recognize human faces, and Egyptians embalmed their dead in honey. In Peru, armadillo shells are made into mandolins. Elephants hold funerals. Years after an elephant dies, its family visits its bones and touches its tusks in remembrance. In South America—and this you want to remember for T.J.—people keep boa constrictors in their houses to eat vermin. Crocodiles swallow stones to reach deeper waters.

"Now go on and tell me a little about your bird," your grandmother says when she gets tired. It's your reward. You tell her a wandering albatross can circle the globe in two months. You tell her the birds are rarely seen on the land. They can stay aloft for ten years.

"Where does he sleep?" she asks.

"In the air. While he's flying."

"Good for him," she says. "I can barely sleep when I'm sleeping."

When you next visit T.J., Margaret's there. He has a new camera with a lens he twists like a combination lock. They're in the backyard and Loretta is stretched out in the dead grass, soaking up sun. T.J. snaps pictures of Margaret spinning cartwheels with the snake in the foreground. You're doing figure eights in a wheelchair on the cement patio. T.J. steals them for lawn furniture. The urge to pop a wheelie comes on like a sneeze, but you're afraid you'll crack your head open in front of Margaret. Her cartwheels are languid handstands. When she's upside down, her shirt falls and shows her stomach. You can't tell if she's wearing the red bra. Before leaving, Margaret asks if you like Texas History, and because you're supposed to say no, you do.

Inside, T.J.'s bed is buried under bags from the mall. The room smells of new plastic. There are records, an Atari with games and extra joysticks, and black T-shirts with iron-on images of pot leaves. A pair of motorcycle boots, a samurai sword, rolls of film for the new camera, a collapsible telescope, and a boom box with three cassette decks. One bag overflows with spiked belts and studded wristbands. A new fifty-gallon aquarium is on the floor and almost as long as his bed. T.J. says it would also make a rad coffin for a kid.

Then, remembering, he snaps his fingers and says he scored you a present. He roots around in the bags and immediately you start hoping for a studded bracelet. He pulls out a Rubik's Cube.

"If anyone can solve one of these," he says, "it's you."

He means this as praise and yet it seems like a low blow. You feel small and isolated, gullible in a way, eager to prove you're not as smart as everyone thinks. You want to smoke and fight and cheat on tests. You want people to call you Big Snake or Radical Rich. You don't want to notice how carefully T.J. peels the price tag off the Rubik's Cube. How hard he works to remove every last bit of adhesive goo. How long it takes, how his patience seems boundless. But you do notice, and for the rest of your life, this will be your benchmark for generosity, for love.

Your father comes home for his two-week leave. On the rig, he works the knuckle boom crane twelve hours a day, so his skin is soaked-leather brown. Except around his eyes. His sunglasses leave a tan line, a bright band stretching from ear to ear; his face looks like a raccoon's in reverse. He tells you a roughneck hooked a shark from the oil platform and promises to bring its jaws home for you. Then he calls your mother at The Kettle and asks for meatloaf and chili and chocolate cake. Later, in the flickering light of the television, with your mother drinking Schlitz from a mason jar on the couch and your father sleeping with his feet in her lap and your grandmother smoking in her chair, you look up *Great White* in the encyclopedia. The entry reads *See Under: Shark*. The *S* volume is almost a year away. You're afraid the grocery store promotion will crap out or that your mother will swear off the whole thing. It's happened before. The ivy-stenciled saucers in the cabinet lack their cups.

The *A* volume falls open to the *Albatross* entry. The book's spine is broken there. You read that British sailors used to kill albatrosses. They made pipes from their bones, purses from their feet.

Your house has a pier and beam foundation that's sinking. On Sunday your father raises the east-facing side with bottle jacks. Then he fixes the toilet so you don't have to hold down the handle. Then he pumps Freon into the air conditioner. You stand behind him, but he won't explain what he's doing. Manual labor is off the table. You'll go to college. You'll have an easier life. When you need something fixed, you'll hire a knucklehead like him. He says, "Why do you think your mother gets those dictionaries?"

When he asks about school, you say you love baseball and you might start dating soon. He roots around in his pocket and pulls out six dollars, the bills damp with sweat, and tells you to buy roses. He tells you to wear a rubber, then tousles your hair. He doesn't ask about T.J. Like a fool, he trusts you.

Your father lies on the couch and says he's just going to rest his eyes, but you know he'll be asleep in minutes. He is. Your mother soaks in the tub. After the pipes in the walls stop knocking, a solemn quiet settles in the house. You're afraid your grandmother has wandered off, but she's in her room knitting. Her fingers move like spiders spinning silk. Her eyes are closed. What difference does that make, you wonder. The house starts smelling of perfume and hairspray. Your mother emerges in a satin dress, a loud floral number that someone left at the motel. While she cooks, you set the table with her china.

Supper is goulash with ground beef and stewed tomatoes. Just as everyone sits down, your father's rig contractor calls and says a crane operator burned up his hands in an accident. Your father asks what time to be at the airstrip for the chopper and thanks him. After he hangs up, no one talks. Your mother pushes back her chair and scrapes her food into the trash and barges out into the clammy night. Your father swallows a heaping mouthful, wipes his face with a paper towel, follows her.

When the screen door claps shut, your grandmother says, "Is everybody gone?"

You want to sneak into your room and listen to your parents fight, but you're afraid of what you'd hear. You tell your grandmother she's not alone.

T.J. ditches PE the next two days, then skips everything the rest of the week. Margaret is absent starting Wednesday. Without T.J., no one hits the ball into the outfield so you work on the Rubik's Cube. You can solve two sides and most of a third.

On Friday, a royally pissed Coach Cantu lectures everyone on personal responsibility. He says there's no baseball today and makes the class run laps around the backstops. A blister opens on your heel, but you feel relaxed to not be in the outfield. You wish Margaret hadn't skipped. You want to show her your bloody sock. In the locker room, Drew Harrell keeps saying, "I kissed her vertical smile," and Tommy Ortiz says, "Who cares? I took her to pound town." Everyone laughs about pound town, then some kids come out of the showers talking about how T.J. stole Cantu's wallet and charged up his credit cards. They say Coach called the pigs. They say T.J. will get arrested and sent back to juvie. Your guts feel slackened, slippery. You wrap the Rubik's Cube in your gym clothes and stash it in your locker. You double-check the lock.

T.J. plays his stereo as loud as possible all weekend. He props speakers in his windows, facing out, and blasts Ozzy through the neighborhood. You flip through the encyclopedia to see if boa constrictors have ears. They do, but lousy ones.

Margaret probably bought everything for T.J. Or his mother sent money from Louisiana. You tell yourself you'll walk down and confront him on Saturday afternoon. Then when you wuss out, you tell yourself you'll go later that night. Then on Sunday. Then you decide to see how Coach Cantu acts on Monday. Maybe he'll cop to finding his credit card and go back to goofing in front of Magnum P.I. When you read to your grandmother at night, she tells you to turn down the television. She means T.J.'s music.

Cantu lets the class play baseball on Monday, but begrudgingly. He spends the hour with his arms crossed, checking his watch. He spits tobacco juice into the dirt. Margaret returns to third base, but never breaks a sweat or looks at you. Just before the period ends, you hear twigs snapping in the brush behind the field. It's T.J. He's climbed into the limbs of a live oak to spy on the game through his collapsible telescope. He's wearing plenty of studded wristbands and two spiked belts. When he catches you looking at him, he raises a finger to his lips: *shhh*. Then he gives you the hang loose sign and you feel yourself exhale. You don't know how long you've been holding your breath.

The first time your grandmother wandered off was last November. Your parents were gone and you'd eaten Halloween candy for supper. When you came out of your room for another Coke, you found the front door open. You almost threw up. Your heart scalded your chest with its heavy beating. Outside, the sky was colored like a new bruise.

You ran through the neighborhood yelling her name. Fighting not to cry. Imagining kidnappers and funerals. You bargained in prayer. You told God that if she was okay, you'd stop leering at the lingerie models in the Sears catalog, stop sneaking over to T.J.'s. The night darkened. Streetlamps buzzed on and mosquitoes came out. Two hours later you were covered in bites, sulking home to call your mother.

But your grandmother was in your driveway in a wheelchair. T.J. sat on your porch, laughing at a story she was telling, something about blue laws and a constable and a six-pack of beer. "So I told him to arrest me or have a drink," she said. "I told him life is about picking the right regrets."

"Speak of the devil," T.J. said when he saw you.

"I was looking for you," you said to your grandmother.

"He's been carting me around in this here chair," she said, patting the arm rests.

“I was scared you were lost.”

“I was,” she said. “I didn’t know if I was washin’ or hangin’. I didn’t know if I was the dog or the tree.”

“Big Chopper spotted her behind Kmart,” T.J. said. “She was too tired to walk, so I snagged a chair.”

“Oh, I was clucking and clucking,” your grandmother said. “I was clucking away but I couldn’t find my roost.”

When someone knocks on the door Monday night, you’re afraid your grandmother has gotten out again. You’re afraid she’s been hit by a car. That you think of her as a dog makes you wince.

But it’s Cantu. He says, “I cleared the air with T.J.”

“He’s coming back?”

“Negative,” he says. “Missed too many days.”

“He can make them up in detention. Billy Haas did.”

“T.J. isn’t wired for school. He’s enlisting. Either the coast guard or the navy. He likes the water.”

Bullshit, you think. That’s just T.J. talking, like when he lies about fucking Mrs. Borden in the teachers’ lounge. You’re disappointed that Cantu believes him, and you feel the dismal vertigo that comes with knowing more than someone else. You imagine T.J. laughing at Cantu. Maybe he’s watching from his window right now. Maybe Margaret’s there, too. For a moment, you hate them both.

“Do you want to come inside?” you ask. “We have leftover goulash.”

“You haven’t swung at a ball this whole unit. If you don’t, I’m stuck giving you a zero.”

"I'm scared," you say, like you'd been waiting to tell him your whole life.

"I know," he says.

"Of getting hit with the ball, I mean."

"You solve that problem by hitting the ball first."

Ozzy is blaring from T.J.'s speakers again. The night is packed tight with humidity. A low fog is rolling in, giving you a headache, and you wish you were anywhere but here. Somewhere, you think, houses are covered in ice. You've never seen snow, and you're afraid you never will. If T.J. sails to the Antarctic Ocean, he stands a good chance of spotting an albatross.

"Sometimes T.J. lies," you say.

"Preaching to the choir."

"The coast guard won't let you keep a snake," you say. "The navy either."

"Which reminds me," Cantu says, "let's leave the Rubik's Cube in your locker from here on out."

The next day, Margaret writes nonstop in Texas History. She only pauses to shake ink into her pen and flex her fingers. The lesson covers the experiment where Jefferson Davis had seventy-seven camels shipped to Texas from the Mediterranean. He thought they'd make better pack animals than mules because they could last longer without food and water, walk farther without rest. The camels were corralled at Camp Verde near San Antonio, and their first caravan to and from California was an unmitigated success. Then the Civil War started and no one cared about camels anymore. Some were stolen and sold into circuses in Mexico. Others moseyed off into the

Hill Country. The last sighting was in 1940. You plan to look them up in the encyclopedia tonight, maybe learn something interesting to tell Margaret. You didn't know she had such a thing for camels. You lean forward to read the notes she's been taking but can't decipher her manly cursive. Then she raises her hand, asks for a hall pass, and dashes from the room like she's sick. Her notebook lies open on her desk and you see she hasn't been scribbling about camels at all. The same words command every line: *Have mercy on me, O God, according to your steadfast love, blot out my transgressions.*

Margaret doesn't return to Texas History and PE is half done before she mopes onto the field. She's with Mr. Gutierrez, the vice principal, and wearing school clothes, not her gym shorts and Young Life shirt. You haven't gone to bat yet, you're up next, so seeing Margaret and Gutierrez tightens the knots in your stomach. What you think is that Margaret's confessed to stealing Cantu's credit card. She's come to apologize. You realize you've started accepting the idea of T.J. enlisting and now you hope he'll stay. Margaret and Gutierrez circle behind the backstop to meet up with Cantu. They whisper and nod. They turn their backs to you.

Which means you could have let someone else step up to the plate without Cantu noticing. Or let yourself get struck out. Or walked. But, no. The pitcher is Tommy Ortiz—everyone calls him Pound Town now—and when he registers you beside home plate, his eyes bug out and he shakes his head in mocking disbelief. Like he's Mr. Homerun. Like he didn't have lice last year. There's no fear anymore. In its place is bitter, confounding anger. You're furious—at Margaret, at T.J. and

Cantu, at your whole school and town and family, at yourself. Like when you dropped your tray in the cafeteria. Like when your father leaves, like when your mother does. The heft of the aluminum bat in your hands feels like a dangerous kind of permission. Pound Town's first pitch is a joke, an insult, a sorry underhanded lob, but you swing anyway. And you connect. The bat cracks the ball and a perfectly resonant sound rings out, a note so pure and true that you regret not swinging a bat each day of your life. Every minute until now has—and you understand this in a holy way—been squandered. Time slows, slows, slows. The ball seems to stay on the bat longer than should be possible, like it's some delicate thing, an egg being balanced and carried, and then it's launched back in the opposite direction, and it's flying fast and high and far, as if rolling over a dome, over the curved roof of the Memorial Coliseum where they hold the gun expos in Corpus, cresting the top, being drawn inexorably away, all while you're finishing your swing and dropping the bat to the ground. Run, you think. Then you do. Your knees pump like pistons.

Later, after the police search T.J.'s house, the news will report that he left a note. The note won't be released, but pictures of him dressed as a Klansman sure as hell will. Pictures of his room and the stolen wheelchairs and Loretta's empty aquarium. Pictures of his daddy's twelve-gauge. People will say he worshipped the devil, that subliminal messages were imbedded in the music he loved. They will say T.J. planned to shoot Cantu, too, but Margaret had alerted school administrators and saved the coach's life. They'll say he did it in Cantu's office, in front of the Magnum P.I. glossy. They'll say wet chunks of his scalp fell from the ceiling panels. They'll say T.J. is why Cantu retired early and why Margaret turned into a stoner and why you quit school. They'll say he's why the rig contractor let you lie about your age. For years you can almost believe you've forgotten about him. But in the chopper that delivers you to the oil platform, the water occasionally looks like sky. The sunlight blurs the horizon and banks off the mottled waves at cruel, unexpected angles. In those moments, a shark swimming close to the surface will resemble the silhouette of an enormous bird, and the apparition will recall the year you longed to see an albatross. That sleight of association will bring T.J. back. How he bought you a gift. How he peeled the price tag off as carefully as a parent. How blind you're still afraid you were.

But your world hasn't been torn down the middle yet; that won't happen until the final bell of the day rings. The hours float by and you bask in their luster. Attention is paid to you in the hallways, like you're a transfer student, someone wholly new and unknown. Watchable, that's how you feel. Imminently watchable. Had a cheerleader stopped you in the cafeteria and slid her tongue into your ear you wouldn't have been fazed.

Nor is it a shock to find T.J. in the empty locker room during sixth period. You'd finished the numerators and denominators worksheet in Algebra, then told Mrs. Lemley you needed to use the bathroom. Really you want to fish for compliments from Cantu. This is his off period, and you figure that if you catch him alone, he might praise your swing or recruit you for the baseball team. There's no question that a place on the team would result in some kissing. A duffel bag hangs on T.J.'s shoulder. He's pacing in front of Cantu's office. His presence seems a good sign.

But T.J.'s shoulders drop when he sees you. He looks pissed and put out, and your confidence curdles. You say, "I was looking for Coach."

"So is the Sorcerer," he says.

"I hit a homer," you say so quickly that it's obviously a lie. Cristina de la Riva fielded the ball just as you reached second base. Then Rod Barecky struck out and ended the inning. Rod Barecky suffers from wanton seizures so you're trying not to hate him.

T.J. peers through the windows of Cantu's office, then checks the clock above the lockers. The second hand clicks loudly. The room smells dank and antiseptic. You're about to elaborate on the home-run lie when T.J. says, "I let Loretta go this morning. Out by Whitney Lake."

Your first thought is that he's trying to shock you, a lie-for-a-lie kind of thing, but you know you're wrong. Your heart goes hot like it does. You say, "You're still enlisting? Even after Margaret talked to Coach and Gutierrez?"

"What does Margaret have to talk to those wetbacks about?"

"I thought she confessed in PE," you say.

"Confessed in PE when? Today?"

You try to think of a way to say no, to say you mixed up your days or it wasn't Margaret at all, but you fail. T.J. rakes his hand through his hair and paces in a tight circle. You want him to say something, need him to. He stays quiet, though, and watching him pace makes you dizzy.

"I would've taken care of Loretta," you say. "I would've kept her until you got home."

"You should split," T.J. says.

"If you want, we can look for her after school."

T.J. checks the clock again, the locker room door, Cantu's office. Then he stops pacing and seems suddenly and completely sapped. The word *deflated* scrolls through your mind. Like he meant to do something and now it's too late.

"Sure," he says. "Sure, good idea. I'll meet you out there."

You want to say you'll wait for him after the final bell so you can walk over together, but you tell yourself to be cool. Don't be pathetic. You tell T.J. his plan sounds rad—that's a word you want to use more, rad—and you start back toward your classroom. The halls are quiet except for the squeak of your sneakers on the linoleum. Your confidence bucks up with every step. In your mind, it seems possible to find Loretta near the lake. Albatrosses can locate each other over great distances. Soldiers saw camels roaming in the Hill Country years after they'd wandered off. The Sorcerer found your grandmother behind Kmart. You remember the sensation of hitting the ball and it feels like a promise. You want to run full-out through the school. There are hours of light left, and it's easy to imagine happening upon a snake in the sun. You're hopeful, ready. You're thinking of where to set up her aquarium in your room. You're thinking of how word will spread through the school that you own a boa, how girls will want to visit, how they'll stand behind you when they're trembling and afraid.

PLAYING THE GHOST

I quit Texas after Lorelei troubled my waters. Ten, fifteen years ago. I drove to New Orleans, then Biloxi and Kansas City, wherever there was Nine-Ball action. If I found a motor court laid out like a horseshoe, I'd rent a room for a week. A month if the pool hall had Gold Crown tables, longer yet if I met a friendly waitress. I'd been hustling in Knoxville for a year before Jesse Vodinh kicked in my door at the Sunset Motel and accused me of throwing games. Jesse was a stake horse with a shaved head and an affinity for butterfly knives. I was alone again, on the plum-colored carpet, when my father told me that he'd seen Lorelei haunting our bayou. I hadn't heard his voice in a decade, maybe more. My ears were humming. Jesse had rung my bell before flicking open his knife.

"Haunting?" I asked my father.

"*Hunting,*" he said. "For them skulls."

He meant to warn me off but might as well have said, Come on home, son. You been gone long enough.

My father was from the Louisiana side of Caddo Lake and afraid of witches. He believed any cat, if allowed in the house, would suck your breath clean out. A loose hog was someone under a spell. Or a sign an heir had died and the family didn't yet know.

He moved to Uncertain, Texas, with my mother, though she soon left him for a tent preacher. I kept thinking we'd move, and he kept thinking she'd come back. We were both wrong. My father took work as a guide on our bayou, showing oilmen where to fish for bluegill and running swamp tours for their families. If he saw a white owl, he'd cut the tour short. If the ghost lights were firing, he'd tell the tale of Feu Follet. My father's voice was quicksand.

Uncertain, Texas, is where you wind up if you're lost. Or aim to be. Cabins and bars and churches. Old Guthrie and Wanda own their bait stand and rent out canoes. Guthrie says, The town's called Uncertain because Caddo Lake spans the Louisiana and Texas border, making the town limits impossible to map. Wanda says, The original township application had a box asking for a name and whoever filed the paperwork didn't know what to put, so just wrote *Uncertain*. Guthrie says, Really ain't nobody knows why.

When I got back, I asked Guthrie if they'd seen Lorelei. Wanda said, Someone stole another rental canoe two nights before. Guthrie said, I thought it was three nights. Wanda said, Who cares—gone is gone.

Lorelei had a barbed wire heart tattooed on her shin. A crescent moon on her knuckle. She spent days collecting feathers and bones and skulls from the swamp. She arranged them in sacred shapes, fashioned them into jewelry. When we started up, one of us would say, "Swamp's easy to get lost in," and we'd meet in the backwater. With her, in those sepulchral bogs, the world fell away, and she taught me how much I didn't know. We always seemed on the edge of something dangerous and irrevocable—love, say, or being caught. Once, we happened upon a copperhead skeleton so pristine it might have been carved from alabaster. Another time, in the black mud of Potter's Point, we found a sharply bowled bone that she identified as a pelvis. She took it home and kept keys in it, loose change.

A ghost light is also called a corpse candle—a luminescent sphere just above the swamp. You can go a lifetime without a glimpse, then one night the water will be ablaze. It hovers, darts, disappears. It can be as mean as a cottonmouth, as mischievous as a child. The closer you get, the farther the light recedes. A lantern flickering across a dark field, a porch lamp burning for someone who isn't coming home.

From above, Caddo Lake looks like a horse galloping westward. The bayou channels are thick with bald cypress, gnarled and twisted and centuries old, and Spanish moss shrouds their limbs like shoals of silver fog. Salvinia is choking the swamp. It suffocates everything below the surface and blots out the sun. Guthrie thinks somebody bought it for their aquarium, got sick of it smothering their fish, and hucked it into the lake. Wanda says, That weed wants to turn Caddo into a prairie. Guthrie says, That'll be the end of us.

Feral donkeys graze in a copse of cottonwood. The branches of a crepe myrtle bloom with cobalt-blue bottles. A poacher had moved into Lorelei's old cabin, a dead gator hanging from a rope in a hickory out front.

Playing the Ghost is a lonely game of pocket billiards. You rack the balls and break, then place the cue ball anywhere on the table for your first shot. Miss after that, even once, and you lose. The ghost never misses.

A few days before Jesse found me at the Sunset, I was racking the balls and explaining the game to a waitress. Her hair was bleached, and she was wearing fringed boots. I hoped she might prove friendly. I said it's like Solitaire, and she said Solitaire used to be called Patience. Witches read the game like tarot cards and told fortunes.

"I didn't think people from Tennessee believed in witches," I said.

"I wouldn't know," the waitress said. "I'm not from here."

"I'm out to make a fortune, not tell one," I said.

She slipped a pen from behind her ear, scratched her address onto a napkin, sunk it in the corner pocket.

Feu Follet is another name for ghost light. The Cajun fairy. My father believed she toyed with fishermen for sport. Guthrie says, It's the burning soul of an unbaptized child. Wanda says, That's pure horseshit. She was sent back by God, meant to be doing penance but turned spiteful. Feu Follet makes folks believe they can catch her, gets them so turned around in the bog they never come out. Guthrie says, What makes you so sure she's a woman. Wanda says, She's a fairy, ain't she? Besides, it's only men who go missing—men and my canoes. Guthrie says,

Maybe men are just stupider. Wanda says, I can shake hands with that.

When we spotted the pelvis in the black mud of Potter's Point, Lorelei said, "Feu Follet strikes again."

The waitress lived in a shotgun shack with her boyfriend. He shook my hand without squeezing and said, "Call me Darkness."

The bottle tree was on the old Guillot homestead. Guillot believed any evil approaching the house after dark would be enchanted by the cobalt glass. Spirits slid inside and were trapped, then seared by the sunrise. When breezes came through the marsh, the bottles whistled—the last song of the wicked.

At dusk, I found Lorelei admiring the bottles. Her back stayed to me. She touched one bottle, then another, like a child hanging ornaments. Without turning, she said, "I thought you were in Knoxville."

"My father said you'd come home," I said.

She twisted to meet my eyes, bemused, as if she'd caught me lying. Turning back, she said, "Your daddy never liked me."

"He liked you plenty," I said. "He didn't like you being married."

"I'm not married now," she said.

"Wanda thinks you stole a canoe."

"I just cut it loose," she said. "That's not stealing."

A barred owl called from the shadows. Lorelei pivoted to face me. Her gaze seemed a reckoning, like my virtues and trespasses were being weighed against one another.

"Swamp's easy to get lost in," she said.

"Yes," I said.

Darkness wore a starched white shirt, black suspenders. The devoutly dressed hustler. The waitress had marked Jesse Vodinh long ago—he flashed his jellyroll every time he paid for a drink—so they'd been looking for someone to help cut him up. The plan went like this: Darkness would notice me playing the ghost and make a show of challenging me to a race to twenty. I'd accept, but when he wagered five large, I'd say that was too rich for my blood. We'd make sure Jesse overheard, knowing he'd offer to stake me for a percentage. Darkness and I would keep the race tight, but he'd pull away at the end and leave with Jesse's cash. On my way out of Knoxville, I'd stop by the shotgun shack for my half. It should've worked.

In the end, we stole one of Wanda's canoes and rowed into the swamp. We knocked into cypress knees, threaded through their corded trunks. A flock of white egrets stood so close together they might have been a reflected moon. The night was oil black and dusted with stars.

"What happened in Knoxville?" Lorelei asked from the bow.

"I wore out my welcome," I said.

"I was planning to visit you," she said. She was lying, and I was flattered. She dipped her hand into the lake and dragged the surface, water furrowing between her fingertips. "You saved me a trip."

"You've always been patient," I said.

"Tyler," she said. "I'm sure sorry about your daddy."

I leaned into the oars, then again, harder. We displaced swaths of lily pads—lotus flowers swaying as if brushed by an unseen hand.

"How'd you know?" I asked.

"You said he'd told you I was back," she said.

"He did," I said.

"That's how," she said.

After Jesse accused me of throwing the game, he went into my bathroom and washed his knife. The music of running water, the metallic scent of spilled blood. I lay on the plum-colored carpet, hearing my dead father's voice. Jesse killed the lights before he left, locked the door behind him. Come on home, son.

The swamp narrowed. The cypresses closed in. Ragged curtains of moss made for a long tunnel. Water folded over the oars like bolts of cloth.

I said, "So you're—"

"Here," she cut me off. "I'm here. With you."

"And my father?"

"He's around somewhere," she said.

"So then I'm—"

"Right where you're meant to be," she said. "Lost in the swamp."

"I don't know," I said.

"I do," she said, like an apology.

Behind Lorelei, the lake laid claim to the horizon. My bearings were gone. We could have drifted out of Texas and into Louisiana or some dark province rinsed of time and border, of names and other lies.

Beyond the cypress brakes, the swamp opened, and we crossed into glassy water. We floated through stars reflected on the surface. They undulated, then returned to their inauspicious stations.

In the distance, a flickering ember. A candle lit for the dead. On the wind, the scent of a struck match.

"Feu Follet," I said.

"Strikes again," Lorelei said.

I reached for her hand, and she was gone. Or she had never been there at all. Or I hadn't. My vision tunneled, and the distant ember flared, as if being coaxed to flame. I felt certain it would snuff out, and with it, my life. Okay, I thought. Okay, I'm ready. Then, at once, and everywhere, the lake was nothing but spectral light. The balls rolled and spread, caroming off each other. I was terrified. I was fearless. When I dove in, I made no splash. The water cradled my body like a sleeping child, lowered me to the endlessly forgiving silt.

Above, the lake burned, and in the twisting colors, I read a fortune: The dead gator slips its noose and crawls under the porch to await the poacher's ankles, his knees, his throat, then returns to its ancestral waters, sated and magnificent. The lake rises. It spits out our bitter bones, rids itself of every parasite and poison. A white owl flies from the mossy veil. The bottles sing and fall silent. Wanda locates her canoes. She says, Some kid likely played a prank. Guthrie says, I might not have tied them good, I don't know, it's a mystery. Then Wanda hears noise in the brush and says, What's that? Guthrie says, A mystery? It's a question that ain't yet been solved. Wanda says, No, dummy, what's that noise? Guthrie cocks his head, listens. That? he says. That's just a hog rooting around for supper. Wanda says, Ain't that supposed to mean something, a loose hog? Guthrie says, It means someone needs to patch a fence. Wanda says, No there's more to it, an old lesson or truth, something we're surely missing.

MISS MCELROY

Travis didn't immediately recognize the woman pretending to browse the shelves at the Paperback Swap. When he'd thought of Miss McElroy over the last decade, and thinking of her wasn't so uncommon, she was preserved in amber: the young mother in bikinis and Ray-Bans, beads of lake water jeweling her delicate neck. She wore Ray-Bans this day, too, maybe the same pair from before, but otherwise he had to work to see her as the woman she'd been. She reminded him of a bird losing its feathers, diminished and skittish. When the mailman opened the door and the bells clanged, she snapped around like she'd been pinched. She never glanced at Travis—not when she moved from the romance novels to mysteries to westerns, not when she spun the squeaky postcard rack, not when she slipped through the black curtain and into the Back Room, the section of the shop with the nudie magazines.

The Swap was next to Payday Loans in a strip mall on the west side of Corpus Christi, between the community college and Bayview Behavioral Hospital. The air conditioner always needed Freon, so Travis had positioned small oscillating fans around the store. Customers brought in grocery bags of books to trade, mostly bodice rippers and Louis L'Amours, but occasionally a student had a copy of *El Cid* or *Sir Gawain*. Travis had a shelf beside the counter with a label that read CLASSICS FOR CLASSES; he was piecing together an associate's degree himself, taking evening courses when he could afford them. He was twenty-six and had worked at the Swap for three years, though when anyone asked he said the job was temporary. Before he clocked out each night, he loaded his backpack with the most interesting books from that day and sampled them before bed. He lived in the house where he'd grown up, drove his father's old Jeep, had never once left Texas.

The Back Room kept the store in the black. Each day brought a procession of men in tasseled loafers, men in coveralls, men in scrubs. They wanted *Barely Legal* and *Cherry*, *Easyriders* and *Jugs* and *Heavy Metal*. Collectors bought vintage *Playboy*s for the cost of three credit hours at the college. The magazines were in plastic bags, and the bulk of Travis's time was spent watching the video monitor to make sure no one broke the seals. Not that it happened often. Most customers who went behind the curtain took care to avoid attention.

He watched Miss McElroy on the monitor as closely as he watched shoplifters and the bums who came in and masturbated. She flipped through the stock deliberately, as if looking for particular issues, sorting through some mental checklist. More than once, she raised a magazine, inspected it, then deemed it unworthy and moved on. Travis pegged her for a dealer coming to restock a flea market booth. Her hair was tamed into a thick ponytail and sweat had matted loose strands to the nape of her neck, her concave cheeks. She'd lost weight since Travis had last seen her. He wondered if she was sick. She had the room to herself but kept peeking toward the curtain. Every so often, she shook her head like she was trying to keep a thought from gaining purchase. He hoped no other customers showed. He considered flipping the CLOSED sign in the window but couldn't risk an impromptu visit from the owner. When Miss McElroy found a magazine she wanted, she trapped it with her elbow against her body. It was easy to imagine her holding record albums that way as a teenager, before she had Holt. The last Travis had heard of him was that he'd returned from Afghanistan after a third tour of duty. Holt had gotten his GED, joined the marines. His homecoming had made the paper and it tinged Travis with relief and jealousy, both unexpected.

Miss McElroy checked her watch and chose a new magazine every few minutes. Travis zoomed in with the camera but couldn't see the titles. He'd pretend not to notice them when she checked out; he'd give her his employee discount. He wished he'd worn a nicer shirt, wished he'd shaved and splashed on cologne. It was possible she wouldn't even recognize him, but he liked to believe he'd left an impression on her. He wanted to know about her life: Did she still live on the lake? Still swim in the mornings? Was she still a waitress? He'd ask about Holt. He'd engineer a way to mention he was close to earning his degree and unmarried, to remind her she used to let him rub suntan oil on her back.

He'd been so preoccupied watching the monitor that he didn't notice the three men crossing the parking lot. Lunchtime was lousy with businessmen and doctors. When the bells on the door sounded, Miss McElroy froze. She flipped down her sunglasses. The men made straight for the Back Room, of course. They wore green scrubs and had cell phones clipped to their waistbands. One said, "He won't skip his meds again, I'll tell you that," and the others laughed. Miss McElroy hugged her magazines with both arms. She sidled by the men, averting her face. The men snuck glances at each other when she couldn't see, arched their eyebrows in a way Travis resented. He smoothed his hair and straightened his posture. On the monitor, Miss McElroy lingered near the curtain and then kneeled abruptly, vanishing almost completely from his view. He thought she was tying her laces or fanning out her haul to check for duplicates. He cleared space on the counter to tally her purchases.

But when she stood again, she was empty-handed. At first Travis thought she'd slipped the magazines under her blouse, thought he'd have to confront her or rationalize the missing stock to his boss, but he knew she was no thief. He repositioned the camera and found the magazines stashed on the floor under the bins. Disappointment sacked him: She wasn't going to buy anything. She came through the curtain in a rush, passing in front of the counter and through the door without breaking stride. The bells clanged harshly, then quieted. A wave of new heat pushed in. Travis leaned against the classics shelf and decided to double-charge the men in the Back Room for running her off. He watched Miss McElroy jog to her little Pontiac like she was going to be sick. She rolled down both windows and accelerated toward Bayview, a dismal brick building that was nowhere near the bay.

. . .

Miss McElroy had lived near Choke Canyon with her son, and for a week each summer, Travis's parents rented an adjacent trailer on the lake. "That poor gal," his mother used to say, "her son's the only hell she'll ever raise." Holt was mean as a hornet: his father had left them years before, and Travis gathered that Miss McElroy blamed him for her son's transgressions. Holt liked to hide and sucker-punch men coming out of the filling station's bathroom. He took their cash and hucked their keys into the brush on either side of the two-lane blacktop. He set fire to tool sheds. Holt bragged about all of it, and Travis acted impressed and unafraid. He was neither. He spent those weeks sure that Holt would turn on him. The fear of physical pain was draining—he was always bracing around Holt, always flinching—but the real menace was the threat of losing access to Miss McElroy.

She swam each morning, and Travis made sure to arrive early enough to see her climb the ladder from the lake and wrap herself in a Navajo blanket she used as a towel. The pretense was seeing Holt, but he would sleep until noon, so Travis usually joined Miss McElroy at the end of the pier. Thinking of those mornings over the years, he remembered watching surfaces dry—her footprints on the planks, her dark hair, the beads of water on her arms and knees and collarbone. She drank coffee from a thermos. She asked after his parents and about his school year. She talked of life on the lake, her own childhood, her ex-husband. "He'd steal the nickels from a dead man's eyes," she said. Sometimes she seemed melancholy and bitter, while others she laughed in a brash, wide-open way that he worried would rouse Holt. Travis calculated that she was sixteen years older and tried to figure how old he'd have to be to ask her to marry him. She called him "sugar." She deemed him sincere and kind, which he heard as compliments, but she said such traits would make his days hard. If the sun burned bright enough, she'd ask him to rub Hawaiian Tropic onto her back. Her shoulders. Her neck.

All day he waited for her to return to the Swap. He refused to restock her magazines; it would have felt like surrendering. He gave two old spinsters store credit for a bag of Harlequin romances that smelled like cats, and he listened to a young man clad in all black extol—heatedly and at length—the virtues of Tolkien and Black Sabbath. He sold a Bible, a copy of *The Monkey Wrench Gang*, and a stack of *Penthouse*s. Between customers Travis read from an astronomy textbook but had to keep starting over when he realized his thoughts had leapt to Miss McElroy. He wondered if she had cancer, if she ever asked Holt about him. He couldn't remember if she'd been wearing a wedding band. He kept the store open an extra hour, then loaded up his backpack and went home to shower.

He hadn't made the drive to Choke Canyon since those summers with his parents, and then only as a passenger, but even in the heathering dusk, the route returned easily. The air held the reedy scent of the converging Frio and Nueces Rivers. He clicked on his brights as the Jeep bounced along rutted roads that had been cut through blackbrush and prickly pears.

Her crushed oyster shell driveway was empty, and the little Pontiac was nowhere Travis could see. No lights in the trailer, no indication that anyone lived there at all. He opened the mailbox and checked for envelopes bearing her name but found nothing. Weeds knotted the yard. Dead June bugs littered the porch. Travis had his backpack slung over his shoulder, its weight suddenly undeniable. He was clean-shaven in his nicest shirt, his cologne like wet evergreen. He'd always been susceptible to wishful thinking, but wasting all this time and gas was silly even for him. Had Holt jumped from the shadows, he would've welcomed another beating.

The moon hung behind scarves of ragged clouds. A diffused light glossed the lake so that the water took on a cobalt sheen. He swatted away whining mosquitoes, heard the mellow waves sloshing boats against pylons. Without deciding to, he made his way toward the old pier. The knoll was sloped, humidity-slick; he had to sidestep down. A lizard skittered in the grass. The pier's weathered planks creaked as he walked, and a warm breeze came off the lake, dragging in the smell of sweet grass.

When he was near the dock, he heard, "Your backpack makes you look like one of Holt's marine buddies."

He couldn't tell if her voice was coming from ahead or behind, couldn't tell if he'd actually heard it at all.

"But you don't really walk like them, so I just took you for a bill collector," she said. "I'm down here by the way."

Miss McElroy was a few feet out from the pier, treading water black as oil. He could barely make out her features in the moonlight.

"It's Travis Dean," he said.

"I know who you are, sugar," she said.

"That's good," he said, sounding lame. His thumbs were

hitched in his backpack straps, which now made him feel—and, he worried, *look*—young, so he let the bag hang off one shoulder. He said, "You used to swim in the mornings."

"I still do, but I've had a day and wanted to rinse off what I could of it," she said. Then she pinched her nose, leaned back, and dunked her head. Travis heard this more than saw it.

"I came out to see Holt," he said.

"Is that right?"

"I wanted to see how he was adjusting, being home and all."

"You were always kind, sugar," she said. "You were always a bad liar, too."

"I read the article in the paper. I've been meaning to get out here."

For a moment the only sound was water lapping over her arms. He wondered if she was skinny-dipping. She said, "Holt's having troubles. He's been in Bayview for a spell. The doctors don't know when he'll leave. He stays pretty upset."

"I'm sorry to hear that," he said. Despite everything, it was the truth.

"Before they admitted him, he locked himself in his room for a week. I talked to him through the door, left food in the hallway. It was like tending to a rabid dog," she said. "Do you know soldiers wear flea collars around their ankles to ward off sand fleas? I used to send him those."

The dogs of war, Travis thought. Crickets trilled in the near dark. The clouds were unwrapping themselves from the moon and the Milky Way was gauzing the sky. At the Swap, he'd read that each visible star might be surrounded by a handful of planets, a notion he couldn't grasp.

"I thought he was afraid of something outside his room, afraid someone would ambush him," she said. "Turns out, no. He was convinced he'd kill me. I know he wouldn't have, but his mind was made up. Then he stopped eating."

"I don't think he would have hurt you," Travis said not because it was true, but because he wanted to agree with her.

"He likes girlie magazines," she said. "He does charcoal drawings of the women and tapes them on his walls. It calms him. They're pretty, actually, a lot nicer than the photos. But he obviously can't run to the store and buy the latest issues."

Travis's breath caught. The night closed around him. The lake went still. He said, "You recognized me?"

"I'd never seen you there before. Then one of his snarky orderlies came in. I'll have to start buying my *Cheating Housewives* elsewhere."

"Don't be silly. I can give you my discount."

She took water in her mouth, fountained it out. She said, "I always thought you'd leave. I thought you were too smart to stay down here."

"The Swap is temporary," he said. "I'm just a few credits shy of getting my—"

"I'm sorry for whatever he did," she cut him off.

Sweat was tracking down Travis's back. He plucked his nice shirt from his skin. He said, "Do what?"

"Whatever Holt did to run you off. I'm sorry for it. He is, too, in his way. He always looked forward to your visits. We both did."

"My parents couldn't afford the trailer anymore," he said. "We just lost touch after that."

Miss McElroy swam in a lazy circle, stretching out her whole body. If she had resembled a dying bird earlier in the day, she looked sleek and ethereal now, a little dangerous. When she started treading water again, she said, "I hated hearing about your father, sugar. Then about your mother."

Travis thanked her and switched the backpack to his other shoulder. His parents had been on their way to go floundering the night the truck veered into their lane. His father died instantly, but his mother lasted another few weeks. Travis sat beside her hospital bed and read to her from books he found in the waiting room. When he finished those, he asked the nurses where he might find others and they suggested the Swap. It was the first he'd ever heard of the place.

Miss McElroy dunked her head again, then came up and drew breath. She said, "They were good parents. You were lucky there."

"You're good, too," he said.

"Oh, I'm world class," she said. "If failing to buy your crazy son a stack of *Hustlers* is on the ballot, I've got Mother of the Year stitched up."

"Where's your car?"

"My old man ran to get supper. The gas station sells tacos now," she said. "You're welcome to stay."

A bird was calling plaintively from the branches of a persimmon tree, and Travis realized he'd been hearing it all along.

"I need to head back," he said. "I've got work in the morning."

"Another time, then," she said.

"When Holt comes home," Travis said.

"He was sweeter with you around," she said. "I could've dealt him better cards back then."

"My parents just ran out of money. That's all that happened."

"Okay, sugar, we'll stick with that," she said. Then she rolled over and started backstroking toward the middle of the undulant lake. Her arms wheeled one after the other and eventually her motion dissolved into the dark.

Travis couldn't say how long it had been since he'd thought of what had happened, couldn't actually recall if it had factored into his family not coming back. He felt like he'd lived countless lives in the intervening years, none of them especially easy or admirable, so everything from his youth had come to seem effortlessly negotiated. What he remembered was that Holt had stolen a johnboat and they'd gone bass fishing. They paddled into the lake until the shore receded from view, and the day passed without a bite, barely a word between them. But as the sun faded, Holt just started talking—about girls and trouble he'd gotten into and how he'd like to move to Corpus after graduating high school, get a machinist job at the army depot. Then he admitted to watching Travis with his mother in the mornings and said his father wouldn't tolerate such coziness when he came back. He wanted Travis to give him his word that it would stop. The dying light mottled the water and the world seemed to be holding its breath, suspended between night and day. Travis felt on the verge of change, too. He was trying to decide if he should tell Holt his father was a coward and crook and gone for good, trying to decide if saying such things would be cruel or kind, to decide which he wanted them to be, but he never had the chance.

Holt swung the oar like a baseball bat. It caught Travis flat in the chest, the throat. The blow knocked the wind out of him, dropped him backward into the water. His eyes were open. The lake tasted like silt. Travis gagged, choked, lost sight of the surface. He was flailing and kicking and tumbling and twisting in water as heavy as concrete. He thrust himself into a hard tangle of roots, got stuck. His chest burned. He tried to cough and had the sense of being caught in a collapsing tunnel, walls caving in and the ceiling lowering fast. His vision splotched, narrowed, blurred. Then he just gave out, all at once hollowed and spent, and he thought—fleetingly—of how this would gut his parents and, he hoped, Miss McElroy. Then the mottled light wavered away.

Now, as he walked up the sloped knoll, the memory seemed even less consequential to Travis, porous and mystifying, nothing more than a story he'd heard but couldn't fully recall. Had Holt jumped in and pulled him up? Had he swam to shore on his own? Were his clothes still drenched when he got back to the trailer or had Miss McElroy dried them for him? Holt might remember it better, but Travis didn't think so. Memory lied as often as it didn't, and what you'd forgotten could shape you as surely as what you hadn't.

He stood on the porch and squinted toward the lake. Soon she'd climb onto the pier, towel off, and make her way to the trailer. Part of him wanted to stay and wait for her like before, but he knew he shouldn't. She'd called him lucky from the water, and she was right. He was lucky to have his job at the Swap, lucky she'd come in today, lucky that events had dominoed him to this moment, this place—the dewy air, the dead

June bugs, the Jeep that would deliver him home. He imagined Holt in his hospital room, his mind at war against itself and his walls covered in miserable charcoal. He hoped Miss McElroy was right about the drawings bringing him some peace.

Travis slipped the backpack off his shoulders and laid it at her door like an old burden. Inside the bag, the magazines she'd picked out that afternoon were still sealed in plastic. The women on those glossy pages were as exposed and beautiful as a human could be, and he realized he'd always thought of them as trapped, suffocating. In three years at the Swap, this had never occurred to him, but now he recognized the force of truth. If Travis was sometimes susceptible to wishful thinking, he was also given to bouts of sentimentality. Making his way to the Jeep, he decided he would put in his notice at the Swap. He would look into student loans. He would look into getting out of Texas.

He didn't immediately crank the ignition. Maybe he was waiting to see Miss McElroy find the magazines, or maybe he suspected that, once he drove away, he would never return to the lake. He only knew he wasn't ready to leave. He rolled down his window and listened to the night noises—the click of insects, the whispering water, the long and easy breeze slipping through the densely tangled woods. The moon was high, wreathed in thin clouds. The Milky Way looked like words someone had tried to erase on a blackboard. Travis didn't think of his parents or the new planets or the mysteries of God or war or suffering. He was only thinking of Choke Canyon. It was just a place he'd visited as a boy, a place he'd barely known, and yet he'd found his way back without so much as a map. He couldn't fathom such permanence. That anything could last, that his life could still surprise him with any kind of reassuring symmetry, was a marvel, an astonishment.

A pair of headlights swung into his rearview mirror. Even in the dark, Travis recognized it as the little Pontiac rattling up the road behind him. He started the Jeep. He dropped it into gear. As the Pontiac passed and turned into the trailer's driveway, Travis extended his hand and waved. Miss McElroy's man was heavy in the gut and beard, holding two sacks of food; he looked like someone who'd seen trouble. He squinted toward the Jeep, harsh and confused, and Travis thought he'd made a mistake in driving out here. He thought he'd stayed too long and was about to pay for it. Still, he didn't lower his hand, didn't betray any fear or pain, and eventually the man conceded a small tentative wave of his own—like they were old acquaintances, veterans of the same war, fellow survivors.

THE BEGINNING OF WISDOM

A section of the newspaper, rolled into a tight cone and flaming at the top, stuck out of the cook's ear the first time I saw him. This was early June, in Corpus Christi, when I was sixteen and had been hired as the delivery driver for La Cocina Mexican Restaurant. The cook was sweating. He sat cross-legged on the stove in the kitchen, eyes and fists clenched, with two waitresses beside him. One of the women was dribbling salsa into plastic to-go cups. The other fanned the blue-black smoke away from the cook's face with a laminated menu.

The night before, I'd called about the job and was told to show up the next morning for an interview. My father made me wear his pink tie, his only tie, though I'd just expected to fill out an application and learn that I lacked adequate experience. Aside from helping out at my father's pawnshop, I'd never held a job. But there'd been no paperwork at La Cocina, no discussion of previous employment. The owner asked if I had a valid driver's license, a reliable car, any moving violations or outstanding warrants. She asked if I was an honest person, and I said, "I try to be." The answer seemed to surprise and please her, then she told me to go into the kitchen and ask if there were any orders yet. She also told me to tell the cook that if another customer complained about the menudo tasting like beer, she'd call immigration.

When the waitress fanning the smoke saw me, she said, "Bathroom's down the hall."

"I work here," I said.

The cook's head was parallel to the floor, the smoke from the newspaper spiraling toward the grease-blotched ceiling. He wore a mustache and a V-neck T-shirt. A half-empty beer bottle sat next to him on the counter; he reached for it without opening his eyes and brought it into his lap. The kitchen smelled of cilantro and eggs and burning ink.

I said, "Mrs. Martinez just hired me."

"You're white," the other waitress said. Her eyebrows were penciled on. Both women looked tired to me, fierce and old. She said, "Ay, dios mío. Affirmative action at La Cocina."

The cook mumbled something no one understood. The flaming newspaper made me think of the downtown curio shops where old women rubbed oil on your palms to predict your future.

The cook said, "Am I being fired again?"

"Fired," the waitress said, eyeing the burning newspaper. "Now he's a comedian. Now he's Cheech and Chong."

"I'm the new delivery driver," I said. "My name's Julian. Everyone calls me Jay."

"Julian," the cook said. "Julian, what kind of car do you drive?"

"A Cadillac," I said. The waitresses glared at me. I saw that the one holding the menu was a lifetime younger than I'd originally thought. It occurred to me that she was the other woman's daughter. My father's tie suddenly felt tight around my neck. An hour earlier, he'd tied it on himself in the mirror, then loosened the knot and slipped it over my head. Now I wished I'd left it in the car. I said, "It's a convertible Fleetwood."

"The king of the Cadillac line," the cook said.

"Exactly."

"Julian, when I own this restaurant—"

"Ay, dios mío," the older waitress said and took her tray of salsa cups out of the kitchen. Her daughter rolled her eyes and started fanning the smoke again. Her hair hung in thick spirals, her nails were glittery vermilion. She said, "Carlos, Jay's worked here for two minutes and already you're starting with your fantasies."

Carlos raised the beer to his lips and awkwardly tried to sip without disturbing the newspaper in his ear. I wanted to ask why it was there, but also wanted to act unfazed, like I encountered such things daily. When Carlos couldn't manage a drink, he extended his arm behind him and emptied the bottle into a pot of simmering menudo.

"Julian," he said, "when I buy this restaurant, you'll deliver tacos by limousine."

The Caddy was cream-colored, a 1978 Brougham. Whitewalls, chrome, power windows, locks and mirrors, and leather seats and a retractable antenna. Even at thirteen years old, the Fleetwood wasn't a car my family could normally afford—my father drove a Datsun pickup, my mother a Chevy hatchback—but an old woman had pawned it and when her loan expired, my father brought the keys home. Things had already soured in their marriage by then, but my mother had always coveted a convertible, and my father knew her boss drove one, so he must have hoped that a luxury sedan could turn things around for our family, deliver us to a different destiny.

He was the manager of Blue Water Pawn, and he believed everything you'd ever need would eventually float through the pawnshop doors. My mother's opal earrings and pearl necklace, her espresso machine and electric range and Tiffany lamps, my ten-speed bike and computer, my cordless phone and bowie knife and Nikon camera, all of it had once belonged to someone else, and either the owners or the people who'd robbed them had sold the stuff to Blue Water for pennies on the dollar. My father once paid twelve bucks for an acoustic guitar that had belonged to Elvis Presley, and he gave it to my mother for one of their anniversaries. I'd been forbidden from telling my friends about the guitar, but I regularly bragged about it. Sometimes I lifted it from its fur-lined case and strummed its strings.

That the Cadillac came through the pawnshop surprised everyone except my father, and for a while that surprise buoyed my parents. Every couple of weeks they soaped the car with sponges and waxed it until their reflections emerged in the hubcaps. They took it to open-air restaurants on the Laguna Madre, and on weekends they drove north into the Hill Country with the top down. When they returned the seats were littered with pine needles and mesquite leaves, the floorboards dusted with sand like confectioner's sugar. Once, they stopped at a rest area outside Austin and had someone snap a photo of them with my Nikon. They're wearing sunglasses, leaning on the Fleetwood with the tawny horizon behind them; they're not quite smiling, and you can almost sense that my mother is poised to tighten her scarf around her hair and walk out of the frame for good.

On the second anniversary of the night she moved to Arizona with her boss, my father calmly walked outside and cut the Fleetwood's ragtop into ribbons with my bowie knife. When he came back in, he said, "Pop quiz."

Ever since I'd started high school he'd been quizzing me: Name the capital of Delaware. What was the shortest war in history? Who invented wallpaper? When I botched the answers—I'd never answered one correctly—he'd say, "Time to hit the books." My father had his GED.

I couldn't tell if he knew I'd watched him shred the vinyl, so I tried to act casual. I was also worried he'd ask me about my mother. She called me every other month, but sometimes my father answered before I could reach the phone. I hadn't heard from her in a while, so we were both anticipating her call.

I said, "Ready, professor."

"Tonight's prize is a 1978 Fleetwood Brougham, the king of the Cadillac line."

I didn't know what he'd done with my knife. Maybe he'd stabbed it into the steering wheel or one of the whitewalls. My father twirled the keys around his finger. He'd been trying to unload the car for two years.

He said, "What's the beginning of wisdom?"

I knew the answer immediately. A bronze plaque with the words engraved on it hung in his office at Blue Water. I said, "The beginning of wisdom is the acquisition of a roof."

"Touchdown," he said and chucked me the keys.

Later that night I walked by his bedroom and heard him crying. His door was closed, but his sobbing was hard enough to carry into the hall. His room wasn't the one he'd shared with my mother—he'd converted the master bedroom into a storage space and pushed his bed into our old study—though when I pictured him, I couldn't help imagining the furniture as it had been before she left. I saw my mother's vanity under the shuttered window, saw my father trying to muffle his weeping with one of her tasseled pillows.

"Jay," he said through the door. "Jay, are you out there?"

"Just returned from my maiden voyage, professor."

For a moment I thought he hadn't heard me. Then he said, "I left the paper on the counter."

I wondered if this was a new kind of quiz. I said, "Ready, professor."

"Roofs cost money. I'd say it's time you found gainful employment."

"Right away," I said. I thought he'd say something more, or that I would, maybe *I love you* or *thank you* or *I'm sorry Mom hasn't come home*, but finally I just walked into the kitchen and read the classifieds. I called La Cocina because a delivery job would afford me more time in the Caddy.

When I'd worked at Blue Water, the man who stocked the Pepsi machine would brag about free lap dances when his route took him to the Fox's Den, and a customer—a young guy who delivered newspapers and always pawned his fishing rod—said he'd twice happened upon married couples having sex in their front yards, but most of my deliveries went to construction sites or businesses where women wore suits and bifocals: banks, other restaurants, a fabric store, a podiatrist's office. Mornings were our busiest time, and there was usually a lunch rush, but by mid-afternoon our phone stopped ringing and Mrs. Martinez tallied our receipts. I swept and watered the potted ivies and ferns behind the cash register.

At the end of my first week I asked Melinda—who *was* Alma's daughter and a year older than me—why we didn't stay open for dinner. She said, "The only ones that come after lunch are wearing suits."

She was wiping down the tables before I flipped the chairs and balanced them on the Formica. When Melinda leaned over to spray the surface, I saw a butterfly tattoo on the small of her back.

"Suits? You mean, businessmen?"

"*Health department* suits," she said. "If we fail another inspection, they'll chain the door."

Before I'd left with my last delivery, Carlos had been chasing a roach around the kitchen, swatting at it with a menu. The stove was gummy with caked-on lard and I'd watched Alma drink from the milk jug before pouring a glass for a customer. I said, "I guess a flaming sports section in the cook's ear could be considered unsanitary."

"Aire de oído. Like an ear infection. The smoke draws it out," she said.

"I know. My father—"

"How do you afford that car?" she interrupted. She was scrubbing the seat of a booth, trying to remove dried enchilada sauce. There were no more chairs to upend, so I was just waiting, watching her butterfly. She said, "Carlos says you sell drugs, Mama thinks you have a trust fund. I haven't asked Mrs. Martinez because she's all pissed."

"How do *you* think I afford it, Melinda?"

She plopped herself into the booth and looked me up and down. I tried to puff out my chest, and hoped she wouldn't notice my ears, which I knew turned red when I got nervous. She sucked in her cheeks, pursed her lips, squinted. Alma rolled a bucket and mop into the kitchen.

Melinda said, "You sell Avon. No, you mug old ladies. No, you're a hot-rodder. You won it in a midnight drag race."

"Close," I said, trying to sound serious. I remembered what my father told our neighbor when he asked about our new riding lawnmower. "I won it in a card game."

She laughed so loud that Mrs. Martinez poked her head out of the office and whipped off her glasses. "Melinda, have you started making the hot sauce?"

"Ya mero," she said. After Mrs. Martinez closed her door, Melinda said, "So, drugs or trust fund?"

Why I answered her the way I did is still a mystery to me. I said, "The car was my mother's. She died two years ago. I inherited it."

Melinda squinted at me again, studied me in a softer way than before. I was waiting for her to react—to accuse or curse me or start laughing again—when Carlos began singing in the kitchen. It was a Spanish song I'd heard playing on his transistor radio earlier that morning. Melinda continued assessing me. I stared at my shoes, at the restaurant's chipped linoleum.

Sliding out of the booth, she said, "Losing that pink tie after your first day was a good call. You look more like yourself now."

"You just met me," I said.

"Does that matter?" she said.

"Maybe not."

"You're cute," she said. "Especially when your ears turn red."

I never repaired the roof on the Caddy, and after weeks of delivering tacos, I'd forgotten my father had ruined it. Summer in Corpus is glomming. Thick, viscous heat, and there's little rain unless a hurricane is churning in the Gulf, so I just left the top down. I enjoyed smelling the baking asphalt, the far-off briny bay. When I saw someone I knew, I saluted them from behind the wheel. Or I turned up the stereo and pretended not to recognize them.

In July, Mrs. Martinez catered a wedding in Portland, the little town across the ship channel. It took me two trips to deliver all the food—two hundred enchiladas, vats of beans and rice, and bags of flour tortillas that I had to stash in the trunk. (A bag had flown out of the backseat on my first trip. When the wind lifted it into the night, it looked like a jellyfish swimming in black, black water.) By the time we'd set up the buffet it was ten o'clock. I'd thought I might drive Melinda home, but she had to serve coffee to the guests. She said, "If you stay, you can ask me to dance."

"I don't know how to dance," I said.

"Then stay and you can ask me *not* to dance."

I spent the next hour pacing outside the reception hall, pretending I'd just married Melinda. I stole glances at her serving flan and leaning over to ask if people wanted decaf or regular, and the simple fact of her knowing my name amazed me. The prospect of meeting her after dessert sent my heart kicking. I wondered if she was a virgin, if she knew I was. I almost vomited into a pot of azaleas.

When I looked up, Mrs. Martinez was standing beside me, telling me to drive back to Corpus and make sure Carlos had locked up. The last time he'd been in charge of closing, he'd polished off a fifth of tequila and pushed each of the refrigerators into the dining area. She said, "Next morning, what do I have? Rotten food and a cook in the hospital with a hernia."

"Can Melinda come with me?"

Mrs. Martinez touched my cheek. She said, "Sweet Jay. Melinda just left."

As I drove back, moonlight marbled the sky and the bay under the Harbor Bridge stretched out like an endless expanse of deep, rich soil. I imagined Melinda riding beside me, her long hair whipping around us. I heard her small laugh that always reminded me of a sparrow bouncing into flight. With the Caddy coasting along Ocean Drive, I could almost feel Melinda reaching for my hand across the smooth seats. I'd only kissed one girl at a homecoming party, and I'd been too nervous to enjoy it. Our teeth knocked and scraped together, and her mouth tasted of meatloaf and wine coolers; after a few minutes of kissing, she fell asleep and I tiptoed out of the room, feeling simultaneously relieved and despondent. I thought Melinda's mouth would taste of cinnamon.

I didn't register the first fat drops of rain that pelted me, thought nothing of the first thunderclap or the shudder of pink lightning or the heavy, muscular-smelling air that precedes a storm. But within a mile, rain was bouncing off my dashboard and drenching the seats and pooling under the accelerator. The windshield wipers sprayed the water back into my eyes and face, and the Fleetwood fishtailed around corners. Out of dumb instinct, I flipped the switch to raise the roof. The hinges lurched and groaned, a low steel-on-steel grinding, and eventually the jagged strips of wet, ruined vinyl flopped down against me. I was a mile from home, but with the blurring rain and the wind pushing water over my windshield, I could only inch forward. I had to pull over when I couldn't see the lanes. The ragtop draped over my shoulders, like I'd gotten stuck in an automatic carwash.

When I unlocked our front door, the phone was ringing. I'd heard it when I was hustling up the slippery driveway, but I'd figured it for the sound of traffic sloshing by. My father's antique grandfather clock—another boon from the pawnshop—was about to hit midnight. For a beat, I allowed myself to believe Melinda was calling, but I knew better. In two years, my mother had never grasped the time difference between Corpus and Phoenix.

When I picked up, I heard, "Julian. This is Carlos, the cook from La Cocina."

I hadn't even said hello. I'd almost fallen trying to answer before the phone woke my father, and I was shivering in my soaked clothes. A puddle formed around my shoes.

"Is everything okay, Carlos?" With the storm, I'd forgotten to check the door at the restaurant.

"I'm calling to say we've never had a better driver. When I own the restaurant, I'm going to give you . . ." His voice trailed off, and it sounded like he was knocking a bottle against his forehead, trying to jog the word he wanted. I thought he might say *promotion* or *raise,* but he said, "A trophy. When I own La Cocina, I'm going to give you the blue ribbon."

My teeth wouldn't stop chattering. I said, "Thank you."

"Julian," he said, "the true reason I'm calling is for a small favor."

A ride, I thought. Through the front window, I could see the Fleetwood parked by the curb. In the streetlamp's amber glow, with the rain streaming over its body, the car looked immaculate and reposed. The upholstery was getting ruined and I was to blame, but seeing the car like that, I felt an inexplicable pride.

Carlos said, "What I need, what I really need, is for you to bring me an accordion."

"An accordion?"

"This is life or death. I truly need this instrument," he said. "I wonder if your mom or dad plays the accordion, Julian. Maybe they have a spare."

"We're not a very musical family," I said.

"Because here's my idea," he said, then took a long pull from his drink. "When I own the restaurant, we'll have girls posing by the door in Santa costumes. They'll wave in customers. Or maybe they'll be naked except for Santa hats, and they'll play carols on accordions."

"The health department might frown on that, Carlos."

He knocked the bottle against his head again, then drained

it and dropped it in the trash. I heard him pop a top with a bottle opener. Sounding suddenly sober and grim, he said, "Julian, you're right. Even with pasties, we'd be in trouble."

"Unfortunately."

"You're an idea man, Julian. Manager material. When I'm the boss—"

The line went dead. I was about to call Carlos back when my father said, "How was the old girl tonight?"

I didn't know how long he'd been behind me. He was leaning against the sink, wearing pajama pants and no shirt. The scar where he'd had his gall bladder removed looked like a centipede on his stomach. I said, "That was Carlos. From work."

"The cook calls you at midnight?"

"He was drunk. He wants an accordion. I told him to check Blue Water."

My father wasn't listening. He was peering over my shoulder, seeing the Fleetwood in the rain. Wet tallow leaves were stuck to its hood like leeches. The tattered roof looked like a busted garbage bag.

Our air conditioner cycled on. I crossed my arms over my chest, which only made me colder.

My father said, "Pop quiz."

"Ready, professor."

He fixed me with his eyes again, then averted them to the car. He said, "What happens when a yacht fills with water?"

The question seemed deceptively easy, so I considered each word individually. Yacht. Fills. Water. But I couldn't think of any answer beyond the obvious one. I said, "It sinks."

"Touchdown," he said. Then he left me alone, trembling.

. . .

Carlos had gone outside after the phone went dead; he thought lightning had struck the shopping center; the floor and walls had jolted, like an earthquake. But there'd been no more lightning, just gusts of wind that blew the rain sideways and sent shallow waves rippling over the dark parking lot. He was about to return to the restaurant when he saw the downed telephone pole, then after he shelved his hands over his eyes, he saw the car smashed under it, heard its weak, droning horn and saw the headlamps shining dimly through the darkness. The driver was a college student named Whitney Garrett, and if Carlos hadn't carried her to his truck and driven her to the ER, she might've died.

I'd taken the morning off to bucket out the Caddy's floorboards, but that afternoon Carlos recounted everything. He was frying flautas, dancing around the kitchen with his spatula and beer. He said, "Cook saves princess, earns handsome reward."

"How handsome?"

"Julian, by the looks of Mama Garrett, I won't need to borrow your accordion again."

"Carlos, I don't own an accordion."

He slid the flautas onto the plate, spooned on extra rice and beans, then rang the bell for Alma to take the order to her table.

Carlos said, "*Yet*. You don't own an accordion *yet*."

But the reward never came. Days, then weeks, passed after he saved Whitney Garrett and still Carlos heard nothing. He called me every few nights to talk while he drank. He asked if I'd enroll with him in classes to become a rodeo clown, and another time he told me the story of catching himself in his trouser zipper and getting stitches. He said, "Julian, that's happened to me *twice,* so please be careful." He told me that as a boy he'd wanted to be a mariachi singer, that his father had owned a monkey that smoked cigarettes. He talked about how he'd spend his reward money—he planned to buy La Cocina as well as a shrimp boat and recording studio, to outfit Alma with a new wardrobe, to send Melinda to college. He asked if I could think of why Mrs. Garrett would promise to visit the restaurant, but hadn't.

"Maybe she's planning something really special," I said.

"If someone saved my daughter, I'd give them the keys to my house. I'd send thank-you cards every morning. I'd call every night and sing them to sleep."

"Why does Carlos always talk about buying the restaurant?" I asked Melinda. We were eating a late lunch and trying one of his new recipes. When he brought out the plates—steak picado in a taco shell bowl—he'd said, *In my restaurant, this dish goes on the menu. The Melinda and Julian Special.*

Melinda dabbed her mouth with a napkin and stared out the window, thinking. The grass across the street was as dry and blond as hay. I felt lucky to be in the air-conditioning, eating food that tasted of beer. The phone rang, and Mrs. Martinez answered, then walked the order into the kitchen. This was my favorite time of the day to look at Melinda, when her lipstick had worn off and her ponytail was loose. I imagined her looking this way just after waking. I wanted to stay in that booth forever.

She said, "Because Carlos is an optimist, like you."

"Like me?"

"He's always jabbered about owning a restaurant. For years he played the lottery, before that it was bingo. Now he thinks this girl's mother will be his ticket. Carlos thinks money will fall in his lap if he just waits long enough."

"And me? What am I waiting for?"

She took a long drink of sweet tea, crunched an ice cube. She said, "Me."

Mrs. Martinez ambled across the restaurant and handed me a bag of taquitos. She said, "To Beechwood Nursery, on Padre Island. Vámonos, before the causeway gets bumper to bumper."

After she'd left I stood and looked down at Melinda. I said, "If I wait long enough, will something happen?"

She took a bite and chewed slowly, staring at me and smirking. "Do you think Carlos will ever buy La Cocina?"

As often as he'd mentioned it, I'd never really considered that possibility, and realizing that I didn't have an answer puzzled me. I felt shamefully confident that he'd never hear from the Garretts again—a month had passed—but that alone didn't preclude him from owning a restaurant. I said, "I hope so."

"Me, too," she said. Then she winked at me. "Plus, if he gets his own place, he's naming it *Melinda's*."

I thought she was joking, but then it clicked. I said, "You're Carlos's daughter?"

"Stepdaughter," she said.

Then, before I could stop myself, I said, "Melinda, I lied

about my mother. She's not dead. She left my father to live with a lawyer in Arizona."

She took another bite, and my palms went clammy. Mrs. Martinez started feeding her plants behind me, though I could feel her leering at us. The phone rang again. I knew I needed to leave before I got stuck with another delivery, but my feet were rooted, like I'd stepped in drying cement.

Finally, Melinda said, "So it all makes sense."

"What does?"

"Your father," she said. "He's another optimist."

Driving to the nursery, I thought about this, my father being an optimist. He threw horseshoes alone in our backyard and listened to Bach suites while tinkering at his workbench. He read books about surviving divorce, and maybe because a book advised it, he'd started writing in a diary that he hid in his nightstand. I'd read a few pages, but then guilt swamped me and I returned the notebook to its hiding place. He'd lectured me on responsibility because I'd ignored the ragtop, and when I told him about Carlos saving Whitney Garrett, he said, "I hope she *wanted* to be saved."

Roundtrip, the delivery took me two hours because there'd been an accident on the causeway. By the time I made it back to La Cocina, the health inspector had come and gone. The restaurant was empty, the door locked. The CLOSED notice and our failed inspection were posted in the window like new, elaborate menus.

At home, my father was watching *General Hospital*. He sometimes watched soap operas before work, maybe because my mother had watched them. The shows always left him cross. When he saw me, he clicked off the television and asked if I'd been messing with Elvis's guitar again.

I *had* been in his closet, twice in the last week, but I hadn't played the guitar. I'd just wanted to see it. I'd started thinking my father only kept it around to punish himself, and holding the case, I felt sorry for him, and furious; I wanted to cut the strings in half, bash the guitar against the concrete.

I said, "I lost my job today. The health department shut us down."

My father levered himself from his recliner, set the remote control beside the lamp. He said, "Maybe now you'll have time to work on the ragtop."

I nodded. I felt my ears going scarlet.

"So, have you been fooling with the guitar?"

"No," I said.

"It's a collector's item, Jay. I shouldn't have to remind you how much it's worth. When I gave it to your mother, she—"

"Professor," I interrupted. "Have you seen my bowie knife?"

I drove by two and three times a day, testing the lock and pressing my forehead to the window. The restaurant was like a diorama, and the longer I was kept out, the more I wanted back in, the more I felt that I'd never worked there at all. I loitered in the parking lot, hoping Carlos or Melinda would happen by, but they never did and nothing ever changed. The notice stayed on the door, the chairs waited to be lifted onto the tables. Through the windows I watched the leaves of Mrs. Martinez's plants fall to the floor. Eventually, a moving crew carted the booths and tables and refrigerators onto a flatbed trailer; two weeks later, a wig store opened in our space.

When the phone rang one evening, I expected to hear Carlos's slurred voice on the line, but my mother said, "Do you hate me as much as your father does?"

Outside, I could hear him tightening a bolt with his drill. I remembered watching him thrash the ragtop, hearing him cry in his bedroom. In his journal, he'd written, *I hope Jay never loves someone the way I love you.* I said, "He doesn't hate you."

"That's a surprise," she said. "Your father, he's a—"

"An optimist," I said.

"An optimist. That's sweet of you. You're a good egg, Jay," she said. "Do you know when I think about him most? Around an election, when everyone blabs about Democrats and Republicans. Remember? *Republican.*"

Every pawnshop has a code that it uses for pricing—a ten-letter word with no repeating characters—and Blue Water's was Republican. Each letter represents a numeral (*R* is 1, *E* is 2, all the way through 0), so pawnbrokers can openly discuss how much to buy or sell merchandise for without betraying anything to customers. My father had taught us the code years before, so when he said he'd paid *I-N-N* for the Caddy, I knew he'd bought it for seven hundred. I'd tried to explain the code to Carlos one afternoon, and he said, "Julian, you shouldn't discuss politics at work."

My mother said, "I loved hearing the pawnshop guys talk that way. It excited me, a language you didn't hear if you didn't speak it. I still size things up like that. I'll think, Do I want to pay *A-L* for a blouse? Is an espresso really worth *B*? Is *R-N-N-N* too much to send in my Jay's birthday card?"

"I never got a birthday card," I said.

She went quiet. I listened to the crackling on the line, to my father putting up his tools in the garage. He'd been working out there for hours each evening. I'd been dodging him.

My mother said, "Maybe my calling was a bad idea, maybe I'll let you go."

"I'm glad you called," I said.

"That's nice to hear," she said and started crying a little. Once she'd composed herself, she said, "So, the check's in the mail, as they say."

"Thank you."

"And, Jay, when you get your money, treat your father to a fancy restaurant. Or, one night when he's not expecting it, bring him home a steak and asparagus. That's his favorite meal and he'd like you showing up with it."

Outside, our automatic garage door started closing. The light on the driveway diminished, diminished, diminished, and I heard my father run water to rinse his hands with the garden hose.

I said, "I'll deliver it in a limo."

For the two years between my mother's leaving and my father giving me the Cadillac, he intentionally left the keys in the ignition and the doors unlocked. He said he wanted someone to steal the car so he could file an insurance claim. I'd believed him at the time, but after La Cocina closed, I found myself thinking more about it and doubting him. I suspected he wouldn't have reported the car stolen or tried to claim any money; maybe he *did* want the car gone but couldn't bear to get rid of it. My father, I think, was an idealist.

I worked at Blue Water until school started up again. I loaned thieves and addicts money for mounted javelina heads and leather jackets and leaf blowers; I sold stolen pistols to cops and widows and preachers. I listened to men lie about women and fishing, brawling and hunting, and my father taught me how to study a diamond through a jeweler's lens, to see how its imperfections determined its beauty. He quizzed me on how much to pay for solitaires, how low to sell princess cuts. We spoke in code. We skirted the topic of the Fleetwood's roof. In September, troughs of cooler air brought bands of rain in from the Gulf. If I saw thunderclouds carpeting the sky through Blue Water's windows, I'd run into the parking lot and cover the Fleetwood's interior with a tarp. I weighted the corners with dumbbells someone had pawned, and after the rain dispersed, I wadded the tarp into a ball and shoved it in the trunk.

One Friday night—Blue Water's busiest because everyone needs loans for the weekend—I pulled out my tarp and uncovered a bag of tortillas from the wedding Mrs. Martinez had catered in Portland. The tortillas had slipped under the spare tire and were fuzzy with gray mold. My stomach went whispery, my ears burned. I wanted to throw the bag into the street or on top of the pawnshop's roof, but I left it where it was and slammed the trunk shut and drove home.

The phone was ringing when I got to the house, but I didn't answer it. My father had barged into Blue Water's parking lot as I was accelerating away, and I didn't want to hear how I'd disappointed him again. He called a second, third, and fourth time, but I only stared at the receiver. *He'll tell me I'm irresponsible,* I thought. *He'll say I lack discipline.* When I finally picked up, his voice was sharp and deliberate. “Stay there,” he said. “We need to break bread.”

“Will do, professor.”

Five minutes later he called back. I answered by saying, “Still here, professor.”

“Julian? This is Carlos. Maybe you remember me. I used to work—”

“Where are you?” I asked. Then I was out the door.

They lived in a section of Corpus called The Cut, a neighborhood crowded with rusted, broken-down cars and dirt lawns and boxy tract houses. If the stop signs hadn't been stolen, they were spray-painted with looping gang tags. White-shirted men anchored street corners; women sat on porches and rocked crying babies. A German shepherd lunged against a chain-link fence as the Caddy crawled by, and the air was tinged with mesquite smoke, someone barbecuing or burning branches. A young girl was pinning wet sheets to a clothesline. The streetlights were flickering to life when I saw her, and in the darkness, it looked like she was raising long flags of surrender.

Carlos was doing figure eights on a BMX bike in the middle of his street. He looked like a child learning to ride without training wheels. When he saw me, he laid the bike on the curb and sauntered to the Fleetwood. He'd holstered a beer bottle in each of his front pockets and he gave one to me. We leaned against my rear bumper, watching the night sky thicken.

“A toast,” he said. We raised our bottles. “To La Cocina. May she rest in peace.”

He'd been working day labor, taking the bus across town

each morning and waiting outside Home Depot until someone hired him to clear brush or build a fence or fix a toilet. Melinda had started school again, and Alma was cleaning houses. No one had heard from Mrs. Martinez. That day, Carlos had helped a crew dig up a country club yard and install a sprinkler system; he'd worked for fourteen hours, then called me when he came home. He finished his beer and lobbed it at a trash can, missing by a foot. He held his arm in the air like a basketball player after a jump shot and I smelled his sweat. The odor wasn't foul, just that of a body after a day's work. It smelled vaguely of La Cocina, of the last summer.

"A wig store moved into our old space," I said. "It's kind of sad, I guess."

He nodded twice, shoved his hands in his pockets, and stared into the darkness. I guessed he'd visited the restaurant, too, and was remembering the old days, but he said, "If I owned a wig store, I'd have full-bodied mannequins instead of the little heads. I'd leave them naked except for the wigs. That way, when there were no customers, I'd have something to look at besides hair."

"No health code violations in that," I said.

Down the street a man pushing a rickety snow-cone cart argued with a teenager. The teenager whistled a hard whistle, and the man trundled away. I took a drink of my beer and tried to think of a way to ask if Melinda was home.

"Julian, driving the king of the Cadillacs out here was maybe not your best idea," Carlos said. "Two weeks ago, they shot a deaf guy because they thought he was making gang signs with his hands."

I'd heard the story at Blue Water. After the shooting, my father took each of his pawnbrokers aside and told them to be vigilant about background checks before selling guns. But standing with Carlos, I wasn't scared, and I hadn't been afraid navigating the streets. The world seemed random and unknowable to me, but not utterly cruel or terrifying. Sometimes circumstances put you face-to-face with people you never thought you'd see again, and with that possibility in mind, you could make a life.

"Pop quiz," I said to Carlos. I'd turned around and was unlocking the trunk. I said, "Why did I rush over here tonight?"

"Julian, if I owe you any money—"

"You don't," I said. "Guess who I ran into."

I took my tarp out of the trunk. I'd handed Carlos my beer and when I looked up at him, he was scratching his head with it. He said, "Julian, I'm not so good at tests."

"Mrs. Garrett. Whitney Garrett's mother," I said. "She came to La Cocina trying to find you. I was up there, looking in the window."

Carlos swigged from my beer, then swallowed hard and swigged again. He said, "Julian, are you fucking with Carlos?"

"She wanted to thank you for saving her daughter. She wanted to give you your reward," I said. I lifted the case from my trunk and clicked open the latches. In the violet moonlight, the strings shone like spun silk. The fur-lined case looked like a jewelry box.

I said, "For you, Carlos."

"A guitar," he said.

"It used to belong to Elvis Presley," I said. "It's worth—"

"She must have known I love music. Maybe I said something at the hospital."

"Probably," I said. "You were probably trying to take her mind off the accident."

"Carlos knows how to comfort the ladies." He admired the guitar at arm's length, then held it close and strummed an open chord, then another and another. When the notes died away, I suggested he sell the guitar and put the money toward starting his own restaurant. He said, "Julian, I'll never sell this."

"Where are we going?" Melinda said from behind us.

She'd climbed over the door and into the driver's seat of the Fleetwood. Behind the wheel, she looked exhausted and beautiful, just as she had on the day she'd told me Carlos was her stepfather.

"Field trip in the Fleetwood!" Carlos sang.

He jogged around the front of the car, strumming his strings. He set the guitar on the backseat first, then lowered himself in beside it. I sat in the passenger seat. I must have ridden that way when my mother owned the car, but I couldn't recall ever sitting there before. With the night sky starless and heavy above us, those days seemed part of another boy's life. I didn't know what to say, and had I spoken, I wouldn't have recognized my own voice.

Melinda fixed me with her eyes. I thought she was waiting for me to pass her the keys, but even after I did, she kept looking at me.

"Hey, you," she finally whispered. Then she winked and cranked the ignition.

She hung a U-turn and wound her way out of The Cut. She headed straight for the freeway and floored the gas once she hit those clean wide-open lanes. She took the car to speeds I never would, the speedometer needle trembling to the right. The streetlamps whizzed by like comets. Carlos was strumming and singing in the backseat, but I could barely hear him over the engine and the air whooshing around the windshield. Melinda's hair swirled wildly and the scent of her honeyed shampoo wafted. It seemed we were floating.

I'm not sure when I realized she was driving to La Cocina, or when I realized she didn't know the restaurant was gone. Maybe I knew it when she exited the freeway doing sixty and it felt slow as walking. Maybe it was when she braked at an intersection and the speed had left her giddy enough that she leaned over and kissed me so hard and long that drivers behind us laid on their horns. Maybe it was when I looked back, worrying Carlos would be angry, and found him fast asleep, cradling the guitar. Or maybe I realized it when the night sky opened and the rain poured. Before I could stop her, Melinda flipped the switch to raise the roof. I thought of how disappointed my father had been by my neglecting the ragtop and how I'd been avoiding him because it shamed me, too. With the rain drumming on the hood and streaking the glass, I thought of him finding the house empty tonight. I'd never disobeyed him like that before, but now I thought he'd forgive what I'd done, maybe even approve of it. And as a new pristine ragtop eased down and the rain grew quieter and quieter, I saw my father working those many nights in his garage: He's stretching the vinyl taut over the roof's ribs, riveting the corners, oiling the hinges. He's listening to the intricate music of longing and weeping when he must. He's watching the clouds. He's waiting and waiting, whiling away the hours until a storm gathers and his son can appreciate the painstaking labor of hope, the coded, sheltering lessons of sorrow.

TIME OF THE PREACHER

Holland spent Wednesday building a privacy fence for a tiresome academic couple in Barton Hills. Pressure-treated posts, horizontal cedar boards, stained and sealed, it was his third that week. He had another scheduled tomorrow, then a set of deck stairs on Friday, plus bids out on a tree house, a couple of pergolas, and too many fences to count. Now that everyone was marooned at home, they were dumping money into their yards, walling off their neighbors.

Holland was still getting acquainted with being in demand. He was forty-two, living in a gooseneck trailer out by the airport, divorced. He'd started Good Fences right before the world skidded to a stop. Well shit, he'd thought and figured he'd soon be back working the paint counter at Home Depot. In those early months, when folks were only buying toilet paper and hand sanitizer, he occupied himself by building elaborate coops for the chickens he'd found pecking along the gravel shoulder of the interstate. Now almost a year in and the price of lumber near quadrupled, he turned away more jobs than he took.

While Holland was ripping cedar planks on his table saw in the Barton Hills front yard, a man stood on the opposite sidewalk trying to get his attention. When Holland finally clocked him, the man asked if he built skateboard ramps. "Wouldn't know where to start," Holland said with considerable relief. The man seemed skeptical, possibly insulted. He had two poodles on retractable leashes. Liberals, Holland thought.

When he finished the fence, he pinged the academics inside the house. He knotted his bandanna around his nose and mouth despite knowing they probably wouldn't venture outside. Every aspect of the job had been negotiated by text.

And like that, they appeared in the bay window, reminding Holland of meerkats. The husband pointed at the fence and pumped his fist like he'd sunk a difficult golf shot. Beside him, the wife laid her hands on her heart and mouthed, *Thank you.* Holland waved, then felt ridiculous for having raised his bandanna. The husband made a show of brandishing his phone to send the payment. Holland set to loading his table saw into the truck bed and soon felt his own phone vibrating in his pocket. He used a leaf blower to clear sawdust from the manicured lawn.

It was January, warm even for Texas. The day's light was giving up. When he climbed into the truck, he fished out his phone to check traffic and found his screen stacked with notifications: the academics' payment, news alerts about case numbers and vaccine trials, a request for a bid on a patio deck, a message asking when he could start work on the tree house. Holland hardly registered any of it because there was also a text from Mandy, his ex-wife.

Snake at preachers. help?

It had been almost three years. He dragged his palms over his hair and his patchy beard, couldn't recall when he'd last trimmed either. A churn in his bowels. His thoughts firing too fast. He was tired and hungry and read the text again. He dropped the truck into gear.

Mandy had been the preacher's landlord for a decade; her parents owned rentals all over Austin and employed her to manage them. Before she and Holland went bust, he'd done the handyman work. The preacher's house was well south of the river, tucked back on a street with ditches instead of sidewalks. A few lots had never been developed, dense with twisted mesquite and waist-high bluestem grass. At night, deer stalked into the neighborhood to tear up gardens and tug clothes off the lines. The preacher had once told Holland about seeing a buck with a woman's red teddy hanging from its antlers. Holland could still readily summon the pride he'd felt upon refraining from a joke about racks.

Snakes didn't bother him. He liked catching them and feeling them slip from one hand to the other, as if he were letting out rope. He liked watching them vanish in the brush afterward, liked happening upon the sheaths of their shed skins, featherlight and lace soft. Mandy knew he was partial to them, which was undoubtedly why she'd invented the snake tonight. Driving toward the rental, Holland registered a certain surprise that this was the first time she'd baited him like this, then beneath that, the deeper surprise that she'd stoop to invoking the preacher. Mandy wasn't a believer, exactly, but she wasn't a nonbeliever either, so whatever had occasioned the lie had her in a corner. When she'd contacted him a few years back, she was just of a mind to start some static. They'd met at the Little Darlin' and fought about midterm elections, property taxes, their past transgressions. Holland gathered she was arguing with him because the stakes of arguing with her husband were too high. Mr. Tech Boom, Holland thought. Mr. Start-Up.

Holland passed a food-truck court illuminated by a sagging canopy of string lights, then a Bible church with a digital sign that read: TEXT YOUR PRAYER REQUESTS!!!! Rush hour traffic. Bleating horns. Cars blocking intersections. A mobile testing site had taken over the parking lot of a dead mall, and Holland got stuck behind the line of cars stretching out onto the street. He tried to fix his hair in the rearview mirror while waiting to change lanes. On the radio, hotheads debated stimulus checks and mask mandates. The sky purpled.

When he arrived, Mandy's Tesla was in the driveway where the preacher's hatchback should have been. The front door was open and spilling light. The scene had the upending air of aftermath. Like someone had fled. Like medics hadn't had time to close the door after wheeling the preacher out on a gurney. Holland's body flushed with the abrupt, radiating heat of panic. He parked behind the Tesla and bound across the clumpy front yard, trying to remember the shortest route to the closest hospital.

But then Mandy appeared in the doorway, framed in light. Holland halted, embarrassed she'd caught him rushing. At the house less than a minute and he'd already lost ground.

Mandy wore yoga pants, her favorite chambray shirt, a floral mask. She pointed to her face, somberly. He raised his bandanna.

"Those don't do squat," she said. "You'd be better off wearing a paper bag with eyeholes."

"I can turn around," he said. He sensed neighbors watching between window curtains. "I've got chickens to feed."

"Sorry," she said, regrouping. "I've had a day."

"Where's the preacher?" he said.

"Exactly," she said.

Holland followed Mandy through the house, stepping over a doormat: BLESS THIS MESS. The rooms were all but cleared out, and yet smaller than he remembered, more cramped. The air smelled like the inside of a dust-bloated vacuum bag. In the den, the preacher's ratty leather recliner sat opposite the wall where a TV had been mounted; now only a bouquet of protruding cables remained. A single wire hanger dangled in the coat closet. In the kitchen, cupboards were open, a can of peaches on one shelf, a box of instant rice on another. Mandy's sleek leather purse hung by its strap from a cabinet knob. The overhead lights were garish, the kind of despairing brightness Holland associated with police stations.

"He's under the fridge," Mandy said, and it took Holland a beat to understand. He'd already forgotten the pretense of the snake. And now he remembered how Mandy referred to all animals as males. He wondered if she was still in therapy.

"What color?" he asked.

"Brown," she said. She opened the back door and posted

herself beside it, keeping distance. "Or gray. I didn't get the best look. I screamed and ran outside."

"Any black and white stripes on the tail? Any red or yellow?"

She lidded her eyes, a pantomime of recollection, then shook her head. "He's all the color of mud."

"That's the right answer," he said. He kneeled woodenly; his muscles had seized up on the drive. He used his phone's flashlight to look at the bottom of the fridge: a plastic grille near flush with the Saltillo tile.

"You smell like outside work," she said. "You could bottle it and call it Eau de Labeur."

"You saw it go under here?" he said. "How big?"

"Brides would buy it for their husbands by the boatload," she said. "You could retire early."

"I like my job," he said.

"Good for you," she said. "Good for fucking you."

The preacher—mid-sixties, eyebrows as wild and white as old toothbrush bristles, the slightest suggestion of a lisp—had been two weeks late on rent. He didn't use a cell phone and hadn't replied to emails. He usually paid early, so Mandy assumed his payment had gotten lost in the mail or, with the world gone to pot, he'd just lost track of the date. She waited another week. She logged into her bank account to confirm *she* hadn't forgotten depositing his check. She did entertain the possibility he'd gotten sick but talked herself out of it; Sunday services had been online since March. And weren't preachers prone to cautiousness? Preternaturally wise? Driving to the rental, she'd rehearsed how to strike a disarming tone—*I near forgot my own birthday this year! Who can remember anything right now? Not this lady!* She stopped and bought the BLESS THIS MESS doormat as an excuse for dropping by. Even pulling into the empty driveway, she told herself he'd started parking in the garage. She rang the doorbell. Knocked. Checked her phone. Knocked again, harder, with the heel of her fist. When she finally turned the master key, she was already berating herself for not checking on him sooner, already convinced she'd find him stiff on the floor.

"But, no," she said, pacing the kitchen. "The only things left were that ugly-ass chair and the goddamned snake."

Holland was laboring to move the refrigerator. It was wedged between the counter and hallway wall. Each side would only scoot an inch at a time.

Mandy hopped up to sit on the kitchen island and started swishing her feet like a girl on a pier. Still, she kept her distance. She said, "So that's the situation. The world's on fire, and preachers are skipping out under cover of darkness."

"If you had to estimate the size of the snake . . . shoelace or belt or—"

"You don't find that, like, blasphemous?" she said. "That a man of God would just up and disappear, shafting his landlord? What's to keep me from logging into his Sunday sermon and outing him in the chat?"

"He's been in the wind for two weeks, maybe more. I guarantee he took more from the church than from you," Holland said. A kind of doubt was accruing form and ballast. "Right now I need to know how big of a snake I'm liable to find when we lift this fridge."

"Average size," she said.

"Average of what?" he said.

"He wasn't too big. Or small," she said. "Maybe on the smaller side. Maybe a youngster. He's probably not dangerous, but I don't want him making a guest appearance when I'm showing the house."

Holland was stretching over the counter to see behind the fridge. If there was a snake, and if Mandy had startled it, the most likely place to slither for shelter would be under the fridge. It wasn't impossible.

"Younger snakes are more dangerous," he said. "They can't control their venom. They shoot more in."

"Like I said, I didn't get a good look," she said.

Back in March, when it became clear the madness was only beginning, he'd expected Mandy to check in. Each day he thought: Tomorrow. Each week he talked himself out of calling. Borders closed. Field hospitals were set up. College students were throwing parties, trying to catch it, and Holland knew Mandy had rentals by the university. Before long he got spooked enough to drive out to the gated community on Bee Cave Road. If the gate wasn't open, he'd wait to tail a Land Rover in; the drivers never balked. The Good Fences logo on his truck made it easy for them to think he was building a gazebo for a neighbor's pool. He parked out by the stalled new constructions and watched Mandy's house through the field binoculars he'd ordered to sight planes and birds of prey. He listened to the radio, Merle Haggard and Stevie Ray Vaughan, and hotheads saying convention centers might be converted to morgues. Eventually, he spied her mulching a flowerbed while her husband cleaned their gutters. Occasionally he allowed himself to believe Mandy had done her own clandestine wellness checks, but he knew better. He'd just about broken the habit of hoping to hear from her when she texted about the snake.

And now she was standing on the kitchen island, poised to tip the refrigerator back so Holland, sprawled on the tile, could see underneath. Her palms were flat against the freezer. He was actively avoiding looking up her chambray shirt.

From the floor, he said, "If I say, 'Drop it,' just let it go. Don't worry about me, I'll move."

"You already said that," she said. "Just tell me when to tilt it back. I feel like I'm being frisked."

"Okay," he said, bracing, ready to spring to his feet if he saw anything he didn't like.

"Okay, tilt? Or okay you'll tell me when?"

"Tilt," he said.

"Now?"

"Now," he said. "Yes. Go."

Dust bunnies and dead cockroaches. The bottom panel was solid sheet metal, nowhere for anything to slip in. Holland said, "You can let it down."

"He's gone?" she said. She lowered the fridge but stayed on the island. Like they were castaways and she'd sought higher ground.

"You're sure it went under here?" he asked. "You're positive?"

"Hundred percent," she said.

Holland sidled between the counter and refrigerator, squeezed behind it. The space was so tight that his only option was to squat straight down, as if being lowered into a well, and graze his hand over the backside of the fridge near his boots. He shut his eyes to picture what he was touching: six tiny screws fastening a vented panel, the slits thin and tight. To slip inside, the snake would have to be the circumference of a drinking straw. Assuming Holland could even remove the panel, he'd have no room to scramble if the snake struck. A rush of claustrophobia, a sense that water was rising fast in the well. His bandanna made it hard to breathe.

"And there's zero chance of it being red and yellow?" he said, leaning back to rest his head against the wall, eyes shut. "I need you to be real certain on that count."

"I'd recognize a coral snake," she said. He heard her jump down from the island and pad in the opposite direction. "You think I'm dumb, but I'm not."

"I've never said that."

"You say it without saying it." Her voice had gotten louder, clearer, but also farther away. He envisioned her sitting on the threshold of the back door, unmasked, inhaling clean night air. She said, "That was always your method. You're an insult ventriloquist."

"I don't think you're dumb," he said, and it was true. He thought she was selfish and impatient and made a habit of grinding his heart into dust, but not dumb. She ran circles around salespeople, convinced judges to dismiss speeding tickets, and on a lark one summer, she learned passable Spanish by watching Mexican soap operas. Since the divorce, he'd measured every woman against her and enjoyed a surge of futile, misbegotten pride when each came up short.

"But then again," she said, "a preacher left me holding the bag, so maybe I am stu—"

"There's a vent," Holland interrupted, feigning discovery. "He might've gotten inside."

"That sneaky little shit," she said. "I knew it."

Holland opened his pocketknife and used the tip of the blade to loosen the screws. Tedious, halting work. The blade kept slipping, and it took concentration to find the slot again. He imagined Mandy scrolling through her phone, texting Mr. Start-Up or searching for the wayward preacher. Chambray shirt, he thought. Yoga pants. How she believed brides would buy his bottled scent. He wanted to squirrel away every detail that would animate this evening in his recollection. He wanted Mandy to offer up something she missed about the old times. There was only the metallic hum of the refrigerator, the blood marching in his ears.

When he undid the final little screw, he held the panel in place. Sweat in the corners of his eyes, tracking through his whiskers. He reminded himself that Mandy had conjured the snake from thin air, that it was imaginary, a ploy. To what end, though? To call him an insult ventriloquist? With his shoulders lodged between the fridge and the wall, it seemed feasible he'd misjudged the situation, that he'd maybe never trusted her enough, and for that, he'd soon find himself inches from the dull gaze of a pit viper. He wiped his face on his sleeve.

He had to work to get eye level with the vents in the cramped space, finally rolling half onto his back, chin pressed to his chest like he'd fallen down a stairwell. His breath was coming quick and shallow. The image of the snake striking: the pink flash of its diamond-shaped mouth, the rifle-fire snap of its recoil. He could almost feel the slow boil of the venom in his veins. He slid the panel up slowly, incrementally. If he was lucky, he might be able to slam the edge back down like a guillotine. He was overcome with thirst, sandpaper in his throat. He considered refastening the panel and telling Mandy he'd been mistaken, the vents were too tight after all. When the panel was high enough for him to squint inside, what he saw reminded him of a glove compartment in an old Lincoln—black and spacious and empty. He closed his eyes, just then realizing he'd been forcing them open. He was sapped, awash in humiliating relief.

Now who's dumb. Now who's left holding the bag.

When Holland squeezed out from behind the fridge, he found himself alone. Now Mandy's purse lay on the island like a curled-up animal. She'd snuck off to the bathroom, he figured. Or the preacher had returned, or her husband, and she'd intercepted him at the front door. He felt useless, besieged by the seasick awareness of standing alone in someone else's house. The urge to hide. To bolt. On his phone was a text from the Barton Hills woman saying she'd given his information to a neighbor who wanted a skateboard ramp. Holland deleted the thread. He listened for Mandy's voice, for a flushing toilet. He tried to think of anywhere else a snake might hide. He pulled down his bandanna, then pushed and slid and rocked the fridge back into its place. Eventually he went out the back door, stepping down onto the rough concrete slab that served as a patio.

The backyard was bigger than he recalled, and darker. The preacher had once told him that Mrs. Salazar, the sickle-backed widow in the corner house, had shot the streetlamp out with her husband's rifle because the light shone directly into her bedroom. Holland had repeated the story many times. He hoped she was still there, armed and ornery. The stars were splotchy and dim, the weak splatters of a near-empty can of spray paint. And yet there was light enough to see the yard had gone mostly to dirt. Either the deer had defeated it, or the preacher had never run the sprinklers Holland had installed.

"I left the door open in case he slithered out," Mandy said. Holland had to squint to find her under the live oak across the yard. She was in a folding lawn chair. "I'm sorry I abandoned you."

"Do what?"

"In the kitchen," she said, too quick, lest her apology evoke past disappearances. "I started feeling panic attack-y. I carry chill pills these days but left my purse inside."

"I can grab it," he said. Still in therapy, he thought. "Water, too?"

"He took all the cups," she said. "I'm calmer now. I just keep thinking this is the end of the world. A snake in a house previously occupied by one of God's servants didn't exactly help."

"Maybe the snake was raptured, too," he said.

"Or maybe I'm just mourning not making enough bad decisions when I had the chance."

Holland couldn't tell if she was hinting, setting a snare, or saying the first thing in her mind. His eyes were adjusting, and she was coming into focus. Maybe she'd undone a button at the top of her shirt. Years ago, when she'd started static about the midterm elections, they'd wound up at the Deluxe Inn.

"So far," he said, aiming to sound unfazed and open a door, "my worst decision has been adopting chickens somebody dumped out by the airport. It took me a day to catch them. Brahma, they're called. Show chickens. Prize winners. They have feathers down to their toes. I guess their owners couldn't afford to feed them and couldn't bear to eat them."

"That's some depressing shit," she said.

"The chickens might disagree," he said.

"You built them a chicken mansion is my bet."

The stomach-jump of being known. He looked at his work boots in case he couldn't suppress a smile. He said, "Special chickens deserve special accommodations. They deserve towers connected by a covered bridge. They deserve ramps and balconies."

"And I bet you still make your spaghetti sandwiches," she said.

"Everything tastes better between two slices of bread," he said.

A flotilla of clouds skimmed over the sky from the east, pulled or pushed by secret wind. Then, the sucker punch of memory: a decade prior, another backyard, Mandy sitting in another lawn chair while he cut her hair. He'd never done such a thing and was convinced he'd botch the job, but they were trying to save money for—what? Just then he couldn't remember wanting anything beyond her. The next morning they drank their coffee outside and watched a wren deliver wispy clippings of Mandy's hair to its nest.

"Why did I cut your hair? What were we saving for?" he asked.

"Speaking of bad decisions," she said, but fondly. "I spent twice whatever we saved the next day at the beauty shop. I don't know what we wanted. I think you were mad about taxes."

"So you didn't lure me here for a haircut?" he said. "That's not the next bad decision."

"I lured you here to catch a snake. 'Comes with king cobra' isn't a selling point in today's market."

"If you'd actually seen a snake, you'd call the exterminator. Or your husband."

"Exterminators charge for their services, and Wade appreciates snakes less than I do," she said, then shuddered, as if hit by an arctic blast. "He moved so fast! I'm sure I'll have nightmares about him coming—"

"Up through the toilet when you're trying to pee," he said. "It'll never happen."

"And saying that will never be reassuring," she said.

"Snakes can't breathe under wat—"

Mandy started swiping tears from her cheeks. Then she just crumpled and was crying in her hands. Holland wanted to rush to her but knew she'd fumble for her mask and retreat across the yard. It wasn't a reality he'd be able to bear. He surveyed the dirt and rotting fence, then realized the haggard clouds had disappeared without his noticing. The murmur of faraway traffic.

"Fuck, Holland," she said. "I was already worried before I knew you were just wearing a bandanna. Real masks aren't expensive. I'm sure they make sizes to fit libertarians."

"I'm getting by," he said. "I'm doing all right."

"I'm worried you'll get it, obviously, but also that you'll get it and not tell anyone," she said. "And by anyone, I mean me. You're all the way out in the sticks. You're all alone."

"You're really underestimating my chickens," he said. Insects vibrated in the dark, a throbbing chorus.

"You think you're protecting people, but really you're just scared," she said.

"Scared of what?"

"I never figured it out. If I had, maybe we wouldn't have parted the sheets."

"Things can be simple," he said. "Not everything needs figuring out. Not everything needs psychoanaly—"

"What I need is for you to swear you'll tell me if you get it."

"Scout's honor," he said, quick and easy. When she started crying again, he said, "I've got bottled water in the truck. I can fetch your purse and you can take a—"

"It's like everything was on a solid glacier for our entire lives," she said as she blotted her eyes with the cuffs of her shirt, "but now it's breaking apart and we're on our own little pieces of ice and floating away in different directions. Soon I'll be gone or everyone else will. I mean, if you can't count on a preacher to stick it out, who's left?"

"I am," he said. "I'm right here."

"You are," she said. "And you're sweet to rush over even if you think I'm lying about the snake."

"I want you to feel better," he said.

"Maybe I hallucinated him. Maybe mirages are a symptom they haven't announced yet. Maybe I *did* invent him to get you over here and seduce you one last time, but the shitty preacher took the bed. Who knows? Nothing feels true anymore."

The feeling was constant lately, fortitude being corroded from the inside out, but in her presence, he knew some things were still true. Like, he'd already spent a week in July coughing up blood, his sheets so sweat-sopped that he'd rolled onto the trailer floor but found no relief. Like, he was convinced that's where someone would eventually discover him, and he'd spent hours imagining Mandy getting the news but couldn't figure what he hoped her reaction would be. Like, he'd told himself that if he recovered, he'd vie for another chance, that he'd find a way to approach her without suspicion or wariness, that he'd suggest lighting out for Mexico or Canada, just them and the chickens, but now here they were and he was the same old coward.

"I have a drywall saw in my toolbox," he said.

"English, please."

"I can cut into that wall behind the fridge and look for the snake," he said. "No one'll know once it's pushed back."

Mandy leaned forward in the lawn chair, pondering something. A breeze expanded the branches of the live oak, as if the tree were drawing a great breath. A barred owl called from somewhere nearby: Who cooks for you? Who cooks for you?

"People need home offices right now," she said.

"English, please."

"I'll list it as having space for an office, and someone'll rent it, snake or no snake."

"Or I can cut in behind the bottom shelf of the pantry, which might flush him out the way he came in," Holland said.

"If he's not there, we can take the house down to the studs until we find him."

"You're as stubborn as a scar," she said. "Maybe just help me drag that awful chair to the curb on our way out?"

And like that, the night was over. They listened to the owl for a while, then donned their masks and sulked into the house. For no reason beyond extending their time together, Holland dipped into each room as though doing one last pass for the snake. They tried a couple of different approaches at moving the recliner before pulling out the footrest and stretching the chair to its full length, which made negotiating the doorway disappointingly easy. Mandy carried the front end with her back to Holland. He was tempted to crack a social distancing joke, but instead suggested they hoist the chair into his truck bed in case the garbage collectors wouldn't take it. "I'll give it to the chickens," he said. "Or I'll leave it in the truck and put my feet up when I go fishing." Really, he just wanted to offer her a little more help, wanted that memory to ambush her at some point. Mandy thanked him and promised updates on the preacher. Holland promised to call if he got sick. They took a raincheck on hugging goodbye and pledged to grab lunch when life returned to normal, the bald and courteous lies their parting required.

Holland reversed from the driveway, then she did, and he followed her to the stop sign. Even after the Tesla glided silently through its turn and her twin taillights faded, he lingered at the corner. He knew the chickens hadn't eaten since morning, knew he was due early at tomorrow's job site, knew she wouldn't text or hook a U-turn, but his boot stayed on the brake. No other cars on the road. The night pressed against the truck's windshield; the temperature was dropping. He needed to remember anything he'd said to make her smile, anything that might serve as a seed for some future encounter. His turn signal clicked and clicked. The engine idled. The exhaust purled like smoke from a downed plane.

From behind trees and the darkest corners of the undeveloped lots, the deer watched the blinking red light. All twitching ears, flicking tails, delicate ankles. A buck nibbled delphinium, then, still chewing, raised his top-heavy head to scan the area and check on the red light. A doe scratched her neck with her hind foot. Then she froze. The buck's jaw locked. A tremor beneath their hooves, a rumbling motion somewhere. They swung their heads in unison toward the blinking light as it advanced slowly into the dark. In the truck bed, the old recliner jostled, swayed. There, deep under the seat's cushion, the snake—a copperhead, hungry, still gray at five months old—lay coiled and alert. The world was reverberating from every dark direction, a chaos that frightened and confused her, so she curled tighter, made herself smaller. She stared with unblinking eyes into nothingness. She flicked her tongue, trying to decipher the numberless threats in the cold air.

CAIMAN

Your mother wouldn't let me bring the ice chest into the house, so I left it in the garage. Earlier, I'd knifed four holes into the Styrofoam lid. One of them looked like half a star, which I remember liking. This was years ago, a windswept Sunday. This was Texas.

When I returned to the kitchen, she pointed at the sink. She said, "Wash your hands. With soap."

She was breading flounder. She'd been listening to radio reports about that little girl who'd been abducted. So had I. Probably I pulled over and gave that man eighty dollars because I thought it would keep you safe. He was parked under the causeway, a hand-lettered sign propped against the tire of his van, as if he were just selling pecans.

Your mother had flour dust on her neck. She'd already fried okra, boiled potatoes. Soon we would call you to the table and you, our little man, would bolt in like you'd heard a starter pistol. You were seven, a boy who liked bedtime stories with fantastic monsters and twisty, unexpected endings. You liked sneaking up on us. You hid behind closed doors and in the laundry hamper, then jumped out screaming and laughing. You loved the word *maybe*. (*Maybe I'm a kid who's a million years old. Maybe we should be a family with a pet. Maybe someday my eyes will turn blue.*) Your mother swiped her forehead with her wrist. The kitchen was gummy with the day's heat, the windows open. Before leaving that morning, I'd mowed the yard—you helped me rake, you wore your cowboy boots—and now, with dusk coming on, the cut-grass smell was rising and trying to cool everything off.

"She's still missing," your mother said. "Now they think the uncle did something."

I nodded. I'd heard that, too, and if it was true, I thought he'd get killed in prison. But I didn't want to talk about such things.

Instead, I asked, "How's our little man?"

"Worn out," your mother said. "He's napping in his room." I'd been all day at the job site, drawing overtime. On the drive home, I'd seen the man under the causeway and pulled over for a look. Our ice chest was still in the bed of the truck from when we'd gone floundering. I took that as a sign. And he had only one left, which also seemed lucky. I was excited to surprise you, to hear what you'd name it.

Now I said, "I wonder what he'll name it."

"He asked for a dog."

"A pet," I said. "He asked for a *pet*."

"Right, a dog. A cat. A goldfish. Pets have fur and show affection. Pets aren't deadly."

"Goldfish don't have fur," I said. I didn't think she was angry, not really. I took three glasses from the cabinet. "And it's not deadly."

She fixed me with her eyes. "It's an alligator."

"It's a caiman. There's a difference. It's the size of a shoe."

"Not for long," she said. She turned back to the stove. She laid one piece of fish in the skillet, then another. Grease started snapping.

"They're smart," I said, repeating what the man had told me. "They won't mate until the river is high. They make sure there's enough water for their offspring. They build nests."

"They're cold-blooded. They have scales."

"Danny can take it for show-and-tell."

"They bite. They escape. They escape into sewers and terrorize neighborhoods. They eat regular pets."

I laughed at that, but your mother said, "They do."

She flipped the fish in the skillet. The sound of frying started up again like distant applause. She blew hair from her eyes, stood with her hip cocked, holding the spatula. The applause quieted. She slipped the fish onto a plate she'd covered with a paper napkin to soak up grease. She put two more pieces in the pan and watched them sizzle.

She said, "Why would that man take that little girl?"

"We don't know that he did."

"But you think he did?"

"Yes," I said. "I do."

"I do, too," your mother said. "You know she's Danny's age."

"They could still find her."

"But you don't think they will?"

"I don't know, honey," I said.

"I don't think they will."

She lowered the flame on the stove and turned to stare out the window. She was touching her fingertips to her thumb, one after the other, something she did when she was concentrating. The air in the room shifted.

"What would we do if something—"

"It won't," I said. "Not to him."

She nodded, pressed the heels of her palms to her eyes. She said, "We're still getting a dog."

"I know."

"And you owe me a new ice chest," she said.

I poured milk for you but returned our glasses to the cabinet and opened up two bottles of beer. The meal was starting to feel like a celebration, like one of us had gotten a raise or was having a birthday. I found some cocoa mix, stirred it into your glass.

"An alligator," your mother said, shaking her head.

"Caiman," I said.

"You know some husbands bring home candy, right? Or roses or diamonds."

"Their poor wives," I said. "They probably—"

"Tell Danny you caught it," she said. "Tell him you were fishing and you saw it and you caught it just for him."

"You want me to lie to our son."

"I want you to make up a story for him, something with a happy outcome," she said and turned off the stove. She went to the refrigerator and took out the tartar sauce and a salad she'd been chilling. The wind lifted the curtains over the sink and sent a few paper napkins gliding off the counter. Your mother closed the window, and the kitchen went quiet as a secret.

And then, with the wind shut out, we could hear your boots on the floor in the hallway. You were stalking toward us, planning one of your sneak attacks. Your mother sipped her beer. The flour was on her neck—it looked like snow, like a galaxy—and she was smiling a little. I understood what she didn't: You'd been awake the whole time, listening to us. You already knew about the caiman, about the flimsy hopeful story I'd tell, about everything else. The only surprise left was that I *did* believe they could still find that girl. I thought her uncle might prove everyone wrong. Maybe he cooked her favorite meals, played her favorite movies, never touched her. Maybe such extravagant misguided love was still possible. As a baby, you liked putting your feet in my mouth. You'd laugh until you got the hiccups and your toes would move behind my teeth, and sometimes, I swear, I wanted to bite down, to crush your perfect bones and swallow your body whole.

Your mother knelt to pick up the strewn napkins. You were just on the other side of the door now, trying not to giggle and preparing your ambush. Maybe you knew we were onto you, maybe not. I joined your mother on the floor. I felt like we were praying or giving thanks or mourning. The kitchen tile was cool, hard. We were listening to you breathe, waiting for you to strike. We were on our hands and knees, our bodies low to the ground like strange and ancient creatures.

HALF OF WHAT ATLEE ROUSE KNOWS ABOUT HORSES

His daughter's first horse came from a traveling carnival where children rode him in miserable clockwise circles. He was swaybacked with a patchy coat and split hooves, but Tammy fell for him on the spot and Atlee made a cash deal with the carnie. A lifetime ago, just outside Robstown, Texas. Atlee managed the stables west of town; Laurel, his wife, taught lessons there. He hadn't brought the trailer—buying a pony hadn't been on his plate that day—so he drove home slowly, holding the reins through the window, the horse trotting beside the truck. Tammy sat on his back singing made-up songs about cowgirls. She named him Buttons. No telling how long he'd been ridden in circles at the carnival. For the rest of his life, Buttons never once turned left.

A year later, days after Hurricane Celia hit and everyone was digging through soggy debris for ruined photo albums and missing jewelry, an old woman from Corpus called Atlee about a chestnut mare. It wasn't hers. She'd found the horse standing in her fenced backyard, soaked to the bone and spooked. "I think the storm dropped her here," she said. He drove out and threw a rope not around the mare's neck but her hoof, then coaxed her into the trailer with quiet talk and sugar beet. He ran an ad in the paper, hung signs in the feed stores, called every rancher he knew. He named her Celia, and she turned out to be as fine a horse as he'd ever seen, smart and sure-footed. No one ever claimed the old girl. Not something he'd been able to parse.

The most beautiful thing he'd ever seen was the wild horses in Arizona. He'd gone to deliver Celia to a couple in Phoenix; they needed a companion horse for an old blue roan that was cribbing and stall walking. Atlee was going to miss her, and that must have been evident, because after supper a ranch hand said he knew something that would cheer him up, and they drove out to the Salt River. No one knew how long the herds would survive. The state considered them stray livestock and staged roundups without notice or due process. But Atlee saw a hundred horses that first evening. He glassed the mesa with the ranch hand's binoculars and found the animals in the orange dust. They pawed the ground and threw their heads. They clacked their teeth and nipped one another, bucked and gave playful chase. Wind lifted their manes and tails. They bit at each other's knees and reared up and sniffed the air. When one of the stallions caught a scent, maybe of Atlee himself or the truck or the ranch hand's cigar, they broke into a run like nothing he'd ever witnessed. The herd spread and gathered, spread and gathered, one tremulous and far-ranging body, until they came together in a gorgeous line, a meridian dividing before and after.

. . .

Atlee had read of U.S. Cavalry riders being thrown when their horses saw herds of buffalo. Those horses had originally been used for hunting—they'd been taken from the plains Indians—and the whole of their lives had been spent bolting and surrounding animals so the hunters could spear them down. They couldn't unlearn it, so when they saw buffalo, the horses exploded into runs that dumped uninitiated riders. Atlee liked the image of those men on their asses in the dirt, but he hated to think of the horses waiting in vain for the buffalo to fall.

"Or was it right that he wouldn't turn?" Tammy said, fanning herself with an outdated magazine. They sat on a hot porch, rocking in chairs, hoping for a breeze. His daughter drove out to Seaside Acres every couple of weeks. Atlee was wearing his good denim shirt, a leather bolo tie, boots he'd shined this morning or last night or last week or not at all. He was eighty years old and his memory was mostly leaked out. He couldn't remember how they'd gotten on the subject of Buttons. Tammy said, "I thought he didn't like to go right because he'd been going that way all those years."

"Right was the only way he went. They have memories like elephants," he said. "He just remembered turning the one way."

"He was a mean little shit," she said. "That's what *I* remember. His hobby was clotheslining me with low branches. He liked that crippled boy more."

"When this ends, sell the carousel horse to a collector if you don't want it."

"You say that every visit," she said.

"Let people fight over him at an auction."

"And you didn't pay that man no money for Buttons," she said. "That's just the story we gave Mama. You told him the horse was hurting, and you were confiscating it. You said you could do it one of two ways, but both ended with us taking him home."

Atlee tensed. He always did when Tammy mentioned her mother.

"That was the word you used, 'confiscating,'" she said. "I don't think I'd heard it before, though I've heard it a few times since."

"I know what I said," he lied.

They rocked awhile longer on the porch, then Atlee began the considerable work of standing up. Had the chore not required such concentration, it would have put him in mind of the awkward struggles of a newborn colt, a weak and scared animal, blinking and frightened, feeling his legs for the first time.

A lost horse can follow its own tracks home.

His wife had grown up roping and cutting cattle on a ranch, and the first time he saw her ride—the day Laurel applied to teach lessons at the stables—he knew he was cooked. When she let the reins out and dug her boot heels into her horse's sides, they were nothing but run. "Well, hell," he thought, leaning on the corral gate, watching her. Atlee was twenty-six; Laurel was twenty-two.

"Riding agrees with you," he said as she unsaddled her mare.

"I can teach all of it—western, English, dressage."

"I don't doubt it. You sit a horse well. You've got a soft touch," he said. "When can you start?"

"Really?"

"Yes, ma'am. We've needed a riding teacher for a while."

"No," she said, meeting his eyes. "You really think I've got a soft touch?"

A year later, they had Tammy.

He camped on the banks of the Salt River for two more nights. He ate canned beans from the blade of his pocketknife, drank water from a jug he filled in the river. The wild horses hadn't returned. It seemed a miracle that he'd seen them at all. It seemed a mirage.

Atlee fished and hooked nothing. He sat on the tailgate for hours, swinging and kicking his legs, the weight of his feet in his boots making him feel somehow like a boy. Red-tail hawks circled. Turkey vultures. A bull snake swept across a trail, vanished into the brush. At dusk on the second night, Atlee caught a horned toad and played with him for a bit before letting him skitter away. The clouds were coiled in stars like barbed wire.

The next morning, his last morning there, horses stood on both sides of the Salt River. Atlee had been filling his jug, thankfully downwind, and he stepped behind a stand of oak to watch. They were crossing from one bank to the other, a few at a time. They forded the river effortlessly. They enjoyed the water. Once they climbed out, they shook off and played frisky games, whinnying. He counted twenty of them. Thirty. Forty. Atlee's heart seemed too big for his chest.

. . .

A horse's heart weighs ten pounds.

His own first horse had been a roan quarter horse, his coat so deeply red he seemed to sweat wine. General was his name. His daddy had gotten him in a swap with a farmer. Atlee rode him bareback until he picked enough cotton and baled enough hay to buy an old floppy saddle. General loved to eat dandelions and bark from mesquite trees. Atlee made up a specific whistle, a long high note with two loops in the middle, and when General heard that sound on the wind, he came cantering home. The only time he'd thrown Atlee was when they'd come across a cottonmouth, a thick snake whose head Atlee pinned with a stick and bashed with a rock. When General got colic, Atlee stayed in his stall, drinking bitter coffee from his daddy's thermos. A few times, he claimed General was sick just to spend the night with him. He woke to the horse nuzzling his stomach with his whiskered nose.

He preferred his books and photographs with horses, his movies without. He liked reading about breeds and lore. About the roles they'd played in winning ancient wars and clearing the land that would become the country. About how Plato believed the soul was a chariot pulled by two winged horses, one tame and one wild. With pictures, he liked to see one horse resting its head on another's back. He liked when they looked into the camera with their ears up. (A horse's ears never lie.) Pictures of running horses and horses in snow and horses lowering their necks to drink clear water and—oh hell, the truth was he liked any picture with a healthy horse in it.

What bothered him about movies was what transpired off camera. How they trained horses to collapse onto their shoulders from full runs, to rear up and flip onto their backs. When a horse started running on the screen, Atlee shut his eyes or pretended to pick something off his jeans until the scene changed. He couldn't bear to watch them fall. Once you've seen a horse break its leg, once you've heard that animal scream, it never leaves you.

The carousel horse had been a gift to Laurel. Not from Atlee, but one of her students, the daughter of two lawyers. The girl could ride and her parents took her around the world to compete; there was some hope for the Olympics. They bought the carousel horse at an antiques market in France, shipped it to Texas. Basswood, faded eggshell body, royal-blue and gold and crimson details. It had been on an outside row of the carousel, arrested mid-jump, six feet long. It had a horsehair tail, an elaborately carved saddle and bejeweled bridle, bared teeth and wild eyes and braided mane. The story was that the Nazis were coming through and setting fire to everything, so if carousel owners had time, they dug holes and buried the horses. Atlee didn't know if it was true, but he knew the Germans had killed as many real horses as they could—he'd suffered through *Miracle of the White Stallions*—so it seemed possible. And Laurel loved the statue. Atlee fashioned it to the living room wall and she gazed on it with awe. She was already sick by then.

On that last morning at the Salt River, the colt approached the water countless times. He stepped in ankle deep then backed out or spun and hopped up the bank like a goat. He lost his place in the queue, gathered his nerve, retreated. His body was sheened with moisture. When the colt finally ventured in, it was from a running start, the way Tammy barreled off a diving board. The splash was smaller than Atlee anticipated but big enough to annoy the older horses. The colt labored to keep his head above the current. Where the others were tall enough to walk on the riverbed, he struggled to swim. Atlee wished he had a camera. He wondered how many other people had seen such a sight. He wanted Laurel there, to bear witness with him, to feel what he did: that his whole life had led to this moment, had always been leading here.

Safety matters more to them than food. More than water. More than anything. Lions used to stalk them in the desert. Cavemen chased herds off cliffs for meat. We're predators and they're prey, his daddy said. Understand this and you understand them: Deep down in their blood, they're still afraid.

Once, at Seaside Acres, his favorite nurse asked what scared horses the most.

"The boy's doing a book report," Esther said.

"Just two things," Atlee said. "Things that move and things that don't."

One afternoon at the end of a drought year, Atlee went to the pasture fence and let fly with his double-loop whistle for General. Nothing. He did it again louder. Then again. Heat flared behind his knees and in his temples, and yet he was instantly so cold that his body shook. Another cottonmouth, he thought. Or General was snared in the barbed wire fence, bleeding while flies landed on his torn flesh. Atlee rushed to the tack room. He was gathering a rope and halter, trying to figure what else he might need, when his father told him not to bother. Atlee barely heard him. He filled a jug with sweet oats to shake.

"I sold him," his daddy said.

Atlee stood in the tack room, holding the jug and rope.

"We're belly-up, boy. It was either sell him to buy food or eat horse for a month. I wagered which one you'd cotton to."

There must have been dirt on Atlee's face. He tasted it when the wet ran into his mouth.

Another time, Tammy arranged for a therapy horse to visit Seaside on Atlee's birthday. Well, a pony. He was a pinto with a silly red bow on his tail that Atlee hated. The pony had trouble with the waxed tile floors, so his handler took him out to the trailer and wrapped duct tape on his hooves. It helped. When no one was watching, Atlee untied the sad bow and slipped the ribbon into his pocket. Goddamn, did that horse smell fine.

The crippled boy had juvenile rheumatoid arthritis. Fluid had to be drawn from his knees every other day. He was six or seven, and he'd gone stretches without walking. His parents had called Atlee on the suggestion of Doc McKemie; they needed something for their boy to do that wouldn't tax his knees. Tammy had outgrown Buttons by then, had all but left horses completely behind for baton twirling and talking on the phone, so Atlee told the crippled boy's parents to bring him on out. They wore sandals to the stables. None of them knew not to pass behind horses or to feed them sugar cubes from a flattened palm. But when Atlee hoisted the crippled boy onto Buttons's back, his face lit up like Christmas. And Buttons *did* behave better than he ever had for Tammy. He didn't try to shake the boy off or make a beeline for a low-hanging branch or twist to bite his stirrupped foot. Atlee considered telling the parents about Buttons's orneriness, but he knew it would cost the boy years of rare joy, and he also knew that Buttons would never toss him. The crippled boy's mother took pictures, and weeks later, Atlee received one in the mail. A sun-spotted photo of the boy holding the saddle horn with both hands and an inscription on the back that read, *Maybe mamas* should *let their babies grow up to be cowboys!*

After the chemo failed, then the radiation, Laurel decided against further treatment, her eyes still sharp then. Atlee argued, but she won like always. She was fifty. She lost weight and mobility and much of her sight, forgot her name and how to eat and forgot she was dying, and days came when she did not wake. When she did, she asked him to drive her to the stables. She wept and ranted when he explained he couldn't, so he started lying. He said they'd just gotten back, said they'd gone for a long and peaceful ride in open country, said she'd let out the reins and kicked into her horse and they were nothing but run. She liked that. She went back to sleep smiling.

Want a stable relationship? Get a horse. That was on one of Laurel's T-shirts.

. . .

He didn't see the colt go under. When he couldn't find him with the binoculars, he thought he'd already made it across the river. But then there was a thrashing in the water, as if it had started to boil in the middle where the trench was most deeply cut. The other horses were walleyed, frantic, pushing more quickly toward the far bank like they were being chased. The colt's head breached, then dropped under again. Flared nostrils. Wild, roving eyes. Atlee was on his feet. He was out from behind the trees. In the water. Up to his waist. The horses on the far bank saw him and bolted. He went deeper. He was three hundred yards away, the river heavier and rougher than he'd ever imagined. That he couldn't make it in time shattered him as much as the knowledge, sudden and desperate, that even if he could, he'd be no help.

To bond with a horse, close him in a corral and chase him away. They're terrified of exile, of being cut from the herd, so before long, he'll come up with ways to approach you. For Atlee, the hardest part was acting uninterested when the horse sought him out. That nickering always sounded like a soft apology, always felt like the luckiest of gifts.

Laurel used to say Doc McKemie looked like Willie Nelson. They called him the redheaded stranger. After she was gone, after the stables had been sold and paved over for a shopping center, after Atlee started getting lost in his own house, Tammy drove him to the doctor's office to talk about assisted living. Atlee said, "Turn me out to pasture. I'm long ready." His daughter and the redheaded stranger exchanged a look. They'd expected him to balk. Everyone sat silently for a while. *Don't cross him, don't boss him, he's wild in his sorrow, riding and hiding his pain.*

On Sable Island, far off the coast of Nova Scotia, wild horses survive by eating nothing but beach grass. The island is a narrow crescent, long and harborless, inhabited only by seafowl and the horses. There are hundreds of them. Legend claims they're descended from ancestors that swam ashore after shipwrecks, but really the original horses were abandoned by a Boston clergyman after the Revolution. (Something else Atlee had never been able to parse.) They are shaggy-coated bays and palominos, hardly taller than ponies; over the centuries, their legs have shortened to help with climbing the mucky dunes. Different herds stake claim to different parts of the island. On the eastern coast, fresh water is so scarce that they have to dig holes with their hooves to find springs bubbling beneath the sand. Atlee had dreamed of the island, but of course he'd never visited it. He'd never once boarded a plane.

A band of Mexican soldiers riding north to the Alamo were caught unawares by a blizzard. It stranded them in the mountains. Their horses' noses kept freezing over, so the soldiers had to knock ice from their nostrils. They used the butts of their rifles. Every time Atlee read about it, he heard a thin and beautiful cracking. He saw plumes of warm, desperate breath issuing like signals.

After Tammy left Seaside Acres on that hot afternoon when they talked about Buttons, Atlee was sapped, sullen. He tried to piece the conversation back together, tried to remember if they'd planned a next visit. He skipped supper and Esther came to check on him.

"Looks like someone's got a heart as heavy as a bucket of horseshoes," she said.

He couldn't think of the right words, so he pretended to pick at something on his jeans.

Esther ran her fingers over the carousel horse's carved bridle. Some of Atlee's clothes were draped over it; his bolo tie hung from a wooden ear.

"The boy keeps asking for a pony, and I say, no, sir," Esther said. "I say, when I know half of what Atlee Rouse knows about horses, we'll talk. Until then, the only riding he's doing is the bicycling kind."

Atlee wanted to rest, wanted to be left alone. His thoughts kept floating out of reach, twigs on a fast-moving stream. He said, "Horses were my wife."

"What's that, doll?" she said. "Horses were your life?"

"Yes," he said, "that, too."

A horse that loved tossing an orange traffic cone around his stall. A horse that wouldn't take the bit unless you rubbed honey on it. A horse afraid of anyone wearing a black hat. A horse that would steal your wallet without you feeling it. Laurel's horse.

After a long separation, two horses will put their nostrils side by side and inhale each other's breath; it's their handshake, their embrace, their welcome home. A horse can't see its own nose, but grazing with its head down, it can see the full pasture. Each eye sees a different view, so they're always watching two things at once. To lead a horse out of a burning barn, cover its head with a blanket. It keeps them from panicking. Atlee never had to do this. Thank God above.

Atlee had been too fixed on the colt to notice the stallion. It was in the river suddenly—astoundingly, unbelievably—dunking his head where the colt had gone under. If Atlee's heart had felt too large earlier, now everything about him was too small, too feeble, too inconsequential. There seemed such violence in how the horse dove down, such rage, slamming his head into the water. Atlee heard the thuds. When the stallion came up with his teeth clamped on the colt's mane, Atlee didn't immediately understand what he was seeing. The colt looked diminished, like it had shriveled. Like it had drowned. But he hadn't. The stallion had him halfway between his ears and withers, and he walked him to the opposite shore, not letting go until the colt stood on wobbly legs. The stallion climbed ahead as the colt staggered up the bank. Other horses were still crossing the river, and they passed him, too, but eventually he followed their tracks and was enveloped by the herd.

Atlee stood trembling in the river until the rest had crossed. Then he went back to his truck and wrung out his clothes as best he could. He drove the blacktop highway until he found a filling station with a pay phone. He called Laurel collect. "What'd you do with my tightwad husband?" she joked, but he was already talking. He couldn't wait. He told her about the ranch hand and the first night on the mesa, about the herd's thunderous run, how it reminded him of an infinite flag unfurling, a ribbon of red smoke unspooling and being pulled inexorably away. He told her how he watched them through the lenses, then lowered the binoculars and closed his eyes and listened to them disappear into the fading light, the rumble of their hooves receding like a passing storm. He told her about the bull snake and the horny toad and the colt and the stallion.

"I've missed you, too," she said sweetly, when he was done.

"We'll come back and see them," he said. "We'll visit Celia and bring Tammy."

"You can surprise her when you get home. She'll like hearing how excited you get."

"Yes, ma'am," he said.

But when he got home the stables needed mucking out and one of the quarter horses had colic and part of the pasture fence went down. Then came Laurel's first doctor's appointment, then all of them that followed, then there was too much to talk about and decide, and he never got around to telling his daughter about Salt River. Sometimes, especially after Laurel had forgotten she'd ever heard it, he repeated some of it to her, but never to anyone else. For the rest of his days, it was just theirs—his and hers and the horses'. Then she was gone, and the horses surely were, too, so then it was his and his alone. A passing moment, scattering and shapeless, a story that wasn't a story at all, just something stuck in his head about horses, a memory without beginning or middle or end.

ACKNOWLEDGMENTS

Near the end of Pearl Jam's "Animal," Eddie Vedder screams, "I'd rather be with an animal." His voice is so raw and guttural that the words feel like a kind of feral, desperate plea. Every time I hear it, I think, "Preaching to the choir, Ed, preaching to the choir."

There are, of course, exceptions: Jennifer. Amy (I hate fiction!). Rodney and Lori. Jorie and Peter. Bill (*), Yvonne, Cami (Quarter! Seriously, though: tattoos?), and Julian ("Bro!"). Holly, Joanna, Lauren, Lexy, and Carrie. Jos, Korrine, and Ted. Brad and Brie. Nathan. Austen and Liaht, Jace and Emilia. Liebson. Ben. Big Ryan (We still need to find that *leak*!), Sallie, and Bowen. Jacob, Lilly, Nara, and Karlen. Sieben. Pug and Stevie. Stephen Harrigan. Naomi Shihab Nye. Conor Dougherty. Rob and Jen. Michael Burnett. Mort. Tony and Cathy. Steve and Lucy Enniss. Topher H. Marianne DeLeon. Mark Warren.

These stories—and this writer—would be garbage without the inimitable Andy Ward and everyone at Penguin Random House, especially Julia Harrison, Ted Allen, and the extraordinary Peter Dyer and Madison Dettlinger (Let's skate!). Likewise, Julie Barer and the badasses at The Book Group, and Noah Eaker whose early backing continues to mean so much.

For their generous support, insights, and transformative edits along the way, I'm deeply indebted to: Amy Hempel (I still hate fiction!). Casey Kittrell, Keith Carter, and Holly Doyel. Sven Birkerts. Lauren Aliza Green. Lou Ann Walker. Tyler Cabot. Stacey Swann. Jill Meyers. Linda Swanson-Davies and Susan Burmeister-Brown. Cecily Sailer. Emily Nemens. Ben George. Kathy Pories. ZZ Packer. Don Lee. Andrea Barrett. Heidi Pitlor. Bill Henderson. Geraldine Brooks. Elizabeth Strout. Celeste Ng. Nicole Lamy. Andrew Holgate. Michelle Witcher. Nate Brown. Paul Reyes. No one has offered more love, sweat, and attention to my stories than Rebecca Markovitz and Adeena Reitberger at *American Short Fiction,* and the absolute force of nature that is Allison Wright at *Virginia Quarterly Review.*

Thank you to everyone at the Michener Center for Writers, especially our fellows. Daily I'm reminded what imagination and language, what love and labor, can do. I'm in awe and in your debt.

Finally, it's remotely possible these stories would've been finished earlier if I'd skated less often, but it's a near certainty they wouldn't have even been started if I'd never stepped on a board. For that, and everything else, thank you, skateboarding.

ABOUT THE AUTHOR

BRET ANTHONY JOHNSTON is the internationally best-selling author of the novels *We Burn Daylight* and *Remember Me Like This*, as well as the award-winning *Corpus Christi: Stories*. His work has appeared in *The New Yorker, The Atlantic, Esquire, The Paris Review, The New York Times Magazine, Virginia Quarterly Review,* and *The Best American Short Stories*. He has received honors from the National Book Foundation, a National Endowment for the Arts Literature Fellowship, and The Sunday Times Short Story Award, "the world's richest and most prestigious prize for a single short story." He is the director of the Michener Center for Writers at the University of Texas at Austin.

bret-anthony-johnston.com

ABOUT THE TYPE

This book was set in Minion, a 1990 Adobe Originals typeface by Robert Slimbach. Minion is inspired by classical, old-style typefaces of the late Renaissance, a period of elegant and beautiful type designs. Created primarily for text setting, Minion combines the aesthetic and functional qualities that make text type highly readable with the versatility of digital technology.